THE THORN
IN HIS SIDE

THE THORN IN HIS SIDE

BY

KIM LAWRENCE

First published in Great Britain 2011
by Mills & Boon, an imprint of Harlequin (UK) Limited.
Large Print edition 2011
Harlequin (UK) Limited, Eton House,
18-24 Paradise Road, Richmond, Surrey TW9 1SR

© Kim Lawrence 2011

ISBN: 978 0 263 22250 0

Harlequin (UK) policy is to use papers that are natural,
renewable and recyclable products and made from
wood grown in sustainable forests. The logging and
manufacturing process conform to the legal environmental
regulations of the country of origin.

Printed and bound in Great Britain
by CPI Antony Rowe, Chippenham, Wiltshire

CHAPTER ONE

LIBBY'S phone rang just as she was taking the exit into the motorway services.

She pulled into the first convenient parking space and eagerly reached into her pocket. 'Mum…?'

'Do I sound like your mother?'

Not unless her mum had developed a strong Irish accent in the two weeks she'd been in New York. *'Chloe?'*

'Libby, love, I was just wondering if you're going through the village on the way home from work?'

'Actually, I'm not in work. I'm on my way back from the airport.'

There was a pause before her friend gave a self-recriminatory groan and added, 'Oh, God, of course you are! Sorry, I forgot.'

There was a lot of it around, Libby thought with a worried frown. 'I don't suppose you've seen Mum or Dad, have you, Chloe?'

'Haven't you? I assumed one of them would be picking you up from the airport.'

'They were meant to,' Libby admitted. 'But they were a no show and when I rang I couldn't get a reply…so I got a hire car.' She stopped and shook her head, her smooth brow creasing into an anxious frown. 'It's just not like them, but I'm sure there's a perfectly simple explanation…?' she added, unable to keep the questioning note of doubt from her voice.

'Of course there is,' Chloe responded soothingly. 'And it has nothing whatever to do with ambulances or heart attacks, your dad is fine, and don't deny that's what you were thinking. I know the way your mind works.'

Before Libby could respond to this charge a yawn reverberated down the line so loud it made her grin.

'Why does nobody mention that motherhood turns your mind to mush?' her friend complained.

Libby gave a sympathetic grimace. 'You sound exhausted.'

'I was up all night,' Chloe admitted with another yawn.

'How is my god-daughter?'

'She's teething or colic or something. I've only just got her to sleep. Now how was your trip?'

'Fantastic.'

'And did friend Susie set you up with some gorgeous American hunk?'

'As a matter of fact.'

There was a squeal of delight at the other end. 'Tell me all.'

'Nothing to tell, he was nice but—'

A groan vibrated down the line. 'Let me guess—not your type. Is anyone your type, Libby?' Chloe sounded exasperated. 'Looking the way you do you could have any man—one for every day of the week!'

'You mean I look cheap and tarty?'

'You look about as cheap as vintage champagne, which is why you scare half the men off—too much class.'

'Nice theory but on a more sane note…what did you want me to get you from the village?' Libby asked, stifling her need to get home. Whatever was happening there, five minutes was not going to make that much difference.

'No, don't worry about it, it doesn't matter.'

After a short argument Libby established that the item Chloe needed picking up was Eustace, their accident-prone Labrador, from the vet's.

'Someone left the gate open and useless Eustace got out. I swear that dog was an escapologist in another life. Mike found him tangled up in some barbed wire.'

'Ouch! Poor Eustace, but don't worry, it's on my way, I'll—'

'No, it isn't.'

Libby ignored the interruption. 'It's no bother,' she lied.

An hour later Libby was relieved to see the village come into view. The rain that had made motorway driving a nightmare had finally stopped but the puddles on the narrow country lane where she parked were the size of small lakes. By the time she'd brought the Labrador back to the car her shoes were saturated and her legs splashed with mud.

While the excitable animal strained on his leash Libby fumbled for her keys to open the car door. Her fingers closed around them at the same moment her heel caught in a pothole in the uneven surface. Libby staggered, and, losing her balance in her efforts to stay upright and not land in an inelegant heap in the mud, she lost her grip on the dog's lead.

'Great!' she muttered, maintaining a fixed smile as she approached the dog, who was sitting a few feet away looking pleased with himself.

'Good boy, Eustace,' she cajoled, approaching him slowly with her hand outstretched. 'Just stay exactly where you are…'

The lead was a tantalising inch away from the fingers when he took off, barking madly as he raced away down the lane.

Libby closed her eyes and groaned. 'I don't believe this!' Then she set off after him.

She was panting and had a stitch by the time she

caught up with the errant animal. He was sitting in the middle of the narrow lane, his tail banging like a metronome against the ground as he looked at her with soulful eyes.

'Glad someone's having fun,' Libby croaked as she bent forward, hands braced on her thighs as she tried to drag some air into her lungs. 'Oh, my God, I am so not fit.'

Sweeping wayward strands of her thick chestnut hair from her eyes with her forearm, she straightened up and, tucking her hair in a businesslike fashion behind her ears, took a cautious step towards the dog. The dog barked and took a playful leap backwards.

Libby bit her lip and glared in frustration at the animal.

'I refuse to be outwitted by an animal who even his owners admit isn't the sharpest knife in the box!' she yelled, and thought, You're talking to a dog, Libby.

Worry when you start expecting him to answer back.

The inner dialogue came to an abrupt halt as

her attention was distracted by the sound of a powerful engine. Tractors were pretty much the only kind of traffic this lane saw and this did not sound like a tractor.

It wasn't.

The exact sequence of events hard to recall after the fact, the next few seconds always remained a blur in her mind. One moment she was watching the big black sleek car going at a shocking pace heading straight at Eustace, who clearly thought this was the second phase of the great game, and the next she was there in the middle of the road holding up her hands—it seemed like a good idea at the time—and the car was going to hit her.

When his detour to avoid the snarl-up on the motorway had led him along lanes that were as narrow as they were winding, Rafael had not been unduly concerned. It did not cross his mind to consult the cars inbuilt navigational system or open the road map in the glove compartment. He preferred to rely on his own naturally excellent sense of direction. And it wasn't as if the green lanes of England were dangerous, unlike some of the terrain he had negotiated in his life.

As he drove Rafael's thoughts drifted back to a solo journey he had made at seventeen crossing the mountain ranges of Patagonia in a beat-up Jeep that had broken down at regular intervals until it had eventually been swept away. Who knew that the road he had been driving along had actually been a dry river bed? The recollection of managing to open the jammed door and leap out into the raging torrent seconds before the Jeep had been swept down the mountain brought a wolfish grin to his lean face.

His expression sobered, intensifying the brooding quality of his dark features as he identified the pang in his chest as something approaching envy.

Envy?

Or dissatisfaction?

Rafael's dark brows knitted into a frowning line of impatience over his narrowed cinnamon-coloured eyes. Neither response was either logical or defensible in his opinion—not for a man who had as much as he did.

Rafael attributed in part his uncharacteristic mood of introspection to yesterday's meeting.

A meeting that had not been strictly essential, he need never have seen the man, but to Rafael's way of thinking there were some things that a man, even one as feckless and criminally incompetent as Marchant, deserved to be told face to face, and explaining that he was about to lose his business and his home was one of those things!

He had not expected it to be pleasant and it hadn't been! To see a man, even a bungling idiot, crushed had been painful to witness.

The man had disintegrated before his eyes. A proud man himself, Rafael, embarrassed on the other man's behalf, had found the overt display of tearful self-pity by the Englishman distasteful.

And even though he knew that the man had been the architect of his own misfortune, with a little help from his own grandfather, Rafael had found himself experiencing an irrational flash of guilt as he had taken his leave, guilt that had faded when the other man had yelled after him.

'If you were my son—'

Rafael had cut him off in a bored drawl. 'If I were your son I would have pensioned you off before you bankrupted your firm and lost your family home.'

With a show of more spirit than Rafael had yet observed the man delivered a parting shot.

'I hope one day you lose everything you love and I hope, I *really* hope, that I am there to see it!'

Maybe the words had stayed with him because the curse was uniquely inappropriate?

Rafael had lost the only thing he had ever loved long ago, and the hurt of that loss was now no more than a memory. He had not laid himself open to a repeat of that experience; there was nothing and no one in his life he loved. He could lose all the wealth he had amassed tomorrow and there would be no pain; a small part of him might even welcome the challenge of starting again.

At thirty he had achieved everything he'd set

out to and more. The question now was where to from here?

Rafael recognised that the main problem was how to remain motivated. He was financially successful beyond most people's wildest dreams. A faint mocking smile tugged the corners of his lips upwards. His life was sweet—so sweet that here he was envying the boy he had been, the boy who had led a grim hand-to-mouth existence and relied on his wits and cunning to survive.

Maybe there was such a thing as too much success, he mused, smiling at the irony as he shifted gear to negotiate an extra tight bend in the road.

'So what will it take to make you happy, Rafael Alejandro?'

The harsh curse that was dragged from his lips was seamlessly tacked onto the self-derisive question as out of nowhere a figure ran into the road.

She seemed to materialise in the twilight; for a split second she stood there in the glare of his lights like some ghostly apparition.

Rafael had a fleeting impression of a slight figure, an alabaster-pale face, a cloud of dark red hair; he had no time to register anything else. He was too busy trying not to add homicide to the list of sins recently laid at his door as he fought to avoid the collision, which seemed sickeningly inevitable.

Rafael had never in his life accepted the inevitable.

He had been blessed with catlike reflexes and a cool head when facing danger—and luck, of course. Never underestimate luck, Rafael thought, wondering as he saw the tree ahead if his was finally running out.

It wasn't.

Against all the odds he avoided the suicidal redhead and the tree and remained in one piece. No matter how many times he later reviewed the incident he never could figure out how—it was a miracle!

He might actually have escaped the incident totally unscathed if the car had not at the critical moment hit the patch of mud at speed. Rafael was then forced to sit back helpless as the car went into a dramatic skid that turned the car through three hundred and sixty degrees before it took it across the road and into a ditch. Even the seat belt could not prevent the velocity causing his head to connect painfully with windscreen.

Rafael saw stars through his closed eyelids then he heard voices—no, *one* voice, female and not, he mused groggily, unattractive.

The voice was begging him not to be dead. Maybe he was?

The pain in his head suggested otherwise and the voice sounded too sexily husky to be that of an angel.

Rafael thought, Great voice, stupid questions, and tuned them out while he applied himself to more important matters like was he still in one piece and did those pieces all work?

He took a personal inventory of his limbs. Everything still seemed to be attached and in working order, which was good. His head felt as though someone were playing cymbals behind his eyes, which was less good.

One supportive hand at the back of his neck, Rafael began to lift his head cautiously and heard the voice—the one that did not belong to an angel—murmur a fervent, *'Thank God!'*

He blinked; the action sent a stab of pain through his temple. Wincing, he pressed his hands to his forehead and began to move his head cautiously towards the voice. With equal caution he forced his heavy eyelids apart and through his inter-locked fingers the pale oval of a face swam into view. Hands still clamped to his forehead, fingers pressed to the bridge of his nose, he blinked again and the blurry outline sharpened. The halo of glowing auburn hair seemed strangely familiar, then the rest of her face came into focus.

It was the suicidal female who had caused his accident.

Up close she turned out to be young, beautiful, and his critical gaze could find no flaw in the smooth lines of her face—she was unfortunately a redhead.

Rafael's attitude to redheads was one that had developed gradually, crystallising into a certainty after an incident involving a particularly volup-tuous redhead he had been seeing and a glass of red wine that had ended up in his lap, because apparently he had not been giving her his undivided attention. Redheads, no matter how decorative, were simply too high maintenance.

Even as he was deciding that eyes that blue did not exist without the aid of contact lenses Rafael felt his gut twist as he was hit by a savaging wave of desire that was visceral in its intensity and proved, if nothing else, he was definitely alive, and clearly the message he had sworn off redheads had not reached all parts of his body.

His vision swam again and he closed his eyes, waiting for the wave of nausea to pass. Seemingly these symptoms, along with the uncontrolled rush of testosterone, were results of the head trauma—presumably all would pass.

He opened his eyes just as the redhead was leaning further into the car, her deep russet-coloured hair that reminded him of falling autumn leaves surrounding a vivid heart-shaped face. The nausea had gone. It had been replaced by a reckless and totally inappropriate desire to sink his tongue between those luscious lips.

Even with his scrambled brain working at fifty-per-cent capacity he did consider following through with the impulse, but, *Dios*, that mouth!

On the plus side the lust burning through his veins served as an effective distraction from the hammer pounding in his skull whatever the cause, adrenaline rush and near-death experience…?

A woman's face had not caused him to feel anything this…*primitive* for a long time. Part of him resented what he was feeling—Rafael liked to stay in control of everything including his appetites—the other half suggested he relax and enjoy the moment.

CHAPTER TWO

'ARE you all right?'

Even while he was enjoying the way she smelt, Rafael's critical faculties cleared enough to make him realise this was a stupid question—particularly stupid!

Red-headed and *stupid*, not to mention suicidal. An image of her standing there like a sacrificial virgin waiting for him to crush her under his wheels replayed in his head, releasing a surge of energising adrenaline into Rafael's bloodstream.

'Does it hurt anywhere?' Libby asked, pushing the door a little wider. Leaning inside, she paused, looking around for somewhere to put her phone. She hitched her skirt to rest a knee on the edge of his seat to steady herself as she laid her phone on the dashboard.

'Don't worry, you'll be fine.' She crossed her fingers and thought, Please don't make me a liar.

Fine, Rafael thought, his heavy-lidded eyes trained on the lacy top of her hold-up stocking. He was feeling many things at that moment, but fine was not one of them!

'If I am *fine* it will be no thanks to you.'

Libby was too startled to hear him speak to immediately place the attractive accent of his deep hostile voice, though even hostility sounded amazing when spoken in that voice…a deep and rich purr with a tactile quality that made the downy hair on her arms stand on end.

'I realise that you have to make your own entertainment in the countryside, but throwing yourself in the path of moving vehicles is perhaps a little *extreme*.' Still clasping his head, Rafael rotated his shoulders experimentally and swore as his bruised muscles protested.

Libby's natural response to sarcasm and rudeness, this comment being both, had always been to give as good as she'd got, but given the fact she'd almost killed this man it seemed appropriate to repress such impulses and bite back the retort trembling on her tongue.

'What were you trying to do? Attract my attention? Or is this some local quaint mating ritual?'

Bite me, Libby thought as her initial relief morphed into indignation. Struggling to retain a suitably meek demeanour in the face of this barrage of insults, she mumbled an apology.

'I really didn't mean for this to happen...'

Any attempt to defend herself at this point would only sound lame.

What am I going to tell Chloe?

She began making a silent inventory of her achievements—almost killing a man, smashing up his car and losing her friend's beloved pet, difficult to top, but the way things were going, she thought glumly—who knew?

'I'm so...so sorry,' she said with genuine remorse.

'Oh, that's all right, then.'

Libby felt her cheeks warm with embarrassment in response to the sarcastic drawl as her victim, one hand still clamped to his forehead, turned, head bent forward, and presented her with a view of his broad shoulders and the back of his glossy dark head as he switched his attention to the clasp on his seat belt.

Her glance flickered from the dark hair curling at his nape to the bloody smear on the glass. It was a timely reminder of her role as evil perpetrator while he was the innocent victim.

With a mumbled imprecation she reached for her phone. 'Ambulance…I'll make the call.' Better late than never, Libby.

As she began to speak the man's seat belt freed and he turned. Libby's attempt at a soothing smile dissolved as her lips parted to emit a small mewling gasp of shock, not because the man was injured—she had been prepared for that—but because he was… *He was beautiful!*

From the extravagant sweep of his preposterously long eyelashes to his chiselled cheekbones, imperious nose and wide sensually sculpted lips, he was utterly and lethally gorgeous, but it was the aura of concentrated raw sexuality he exuded that made her stare at him helplessly. Physical awareness clutched like a fist low in her belly and trickled down her spine, making her shiver repeatedly in response to his in-your-face masculine sexuality.

She was so stunned that it took her several moments before she finally registered the cut oozing blood on his broad forehead, a cut that ran from above his right eyebrow and vanished into his dark hairline, and the suggestion of pallor beneath the surface of his even-toned golden skin.

Get a grip, Libby, you've seen good-looking men before—but none this good-looking, said the voice in her head and she could not disagree. He was incredible!

And hurt, a timely reminder. She bit her lip, lowered her gaze and gave a guilty grimace. The forgotten first-aid course had definitely not included drooling while the accident victim bled to death!

'I think…' Libby's voice trailed away. She lost her chain of thought completely as the injured man stared back at her from unblinking tawny cinnamon-coloured eyes set beneath heavy eyelids framed by those long curling lashes that were as dark as his strongly defined ebony brows.

The gleam in his dark eyes as they held her own had an almost combustible quality that intensified the breathless feeling she was experiencing, though maybe it was jet lag—*I hope,* Libby thought, the sensible option pleasing her and scaring her less than the alternative.

She moistened her dry lips with the tip of her tongue and tried again.

'Your head.'

Following the gesture of her fingers, he lifted a hand. He didn't wince but Libby did, her stomach performing a sympathetic somersault as he touched the wound.

He pulled his hand away, glanced with what seemed to her an unnatural degree of disinterest at the red on his fingers before dragging them down the front of his shirt.

Libby, her eyes trained on the red daub, could not help but notice how well developed the chest beneath was.

'Don't panic.' Struggling to follow her own

advice, she began punching the emergency numbers into her phone.

Finger poised above the dial button, she released a shocked gasp as her wrist was captured by long brown fingers. The speed of his action was bewildering but not as bewildering, as the effect the brief contact had on her nervous system.

Libby was struggling to catch her breath when her hand was placed against her heaving chest before being released from an iron grip.

'I do not require an ambulance.'

It was not a statement that invited discussion.

Libby was getting the impression he was not big on discussion. Now orders…oh, yes, she could see him being very comfortable flinging those around. Even after a car smash that would have shaken the toughest customer he retained an arrogant attitude that sent the message he was not someone who was accustomed to having his opinion challenged.

As for the gleam that shone in the darkly fringed intelligent eyes, it was far too perceptive for her comfort, and the flash of something approaching amusement…it was almost as if he *knew* she was trying very hard not to look at his incredibly sexy mouth.

Libby pushed away the whimsical thought, aware that it was her guilt talking. He might not be able to read her mind, but he did have eyes that reminded her of some sleek jungle predator.

'What condition is the car in?'

Libby was startled to see him consult the metal-banded watch on his wrist. It seemed to her that his priorities were seriously skewed.

'I've no idea. I was more worried about what condition you were in.'

A spasm of impatience flickered across his lean face. 'As you see I am fine—in one piece.'

Libby had seen enough hospital dramas on TV to know that people who looked fine and in one piece had a habit of collapsing without warning from massive internal bleeds. While this was not a soap, she did think his attitude was way too casual.

The question remained—how to inject some caution without sounding alarmist?

'Where exactly are we?'

Libby's face fell. It looked as if her caution had been warranted. 'Do you remember what happened?' she asked slowly. Oh, God, what if he had amnesia? 'Do you remember your name?'

'I am not deaf or, as it happens, stupid.' The silent addition of *unlike you* was implicit in the withering look he sent her way.

'I know my name.' He tilted his head towards the window, which offered a view of nothing beyond the grassy bank. 'It is the name of this place I require in order to arrange alternative transport.' As luck would have it his PA was making the journey in her own car in order to attend the meeting he was en route to, which was going to minimise the delay considerably.

'Oh!' Feeling foolish, she lapsed into embarrassed silence as she watched him produce a phone from his pocket.

'There is no signal.'

At last something she did not have to take responsibility for!

'What do you want me to do about it?' She softened the cranky response by adding a pacifying note of cautious concern. 'You might have concussion.'

She could have mentioned a whole host of other injuries he might have, but, not wanting to spook him, refrained—not that he gave the impression of someone who might take fright at the thought of the odd broken bone or two.

Personally Libby, who had never linked laughing in the face of danger with virility, had never been able to understand why so many women were attracted to the action-man macho type.

A bit too much protesting, Libby?

'Concussion…?' He silently conceded the possibility before adding carelessly, 'It would not be the first time.'

'That could explain a lot,' Libby muttered.

On receipt of his narrow-eyed stare, she added with innocent concern, 'I really think you should try not to move.'

The redhead had an abrasive tongue to go with that truly delicious mouth. The irritation Rafael did not attempt to hide was in part aimed at his own inability to think past the sexual hunger still coursing through his body.

As well as the wisdom of avoiding redheads, experience had taught Rafael that a man survived in life by controlling his appetites, not being controlled by them.

'As I have said, I do not require medical attention.'

'It's your funeral.' Immediately wishing she could retract the childish retort, she began to ease herself backwards; she was finding the confines of the car were increasingly claustrophobic.

'I can see you find the thought appealing.'

Libby flushed and protested, 'Of course not!' If she didn't get some air soon she'd be the one needing an ambulance. 'I'm *trying* to help.' Pointless, as he obviously never listened to anyone, she brooded darkly as she continued to edge towards the door.

'I'd feel a hell of a lot safer if you didn't.'

'I've said I'm sorry, and I am, but under the circumstances I think—damn!' Libby slung an exasperated glance at her skirt, which appeared to have caught itself firmly on the gear lever. 'Stupid thing.' She was forced to lean in closer to try and free the tightly stretched fabric.

'Let me—'

His fingers, long, brown and tapering, brushed hers and Libby pulled her hand away as if burnt. She sucked in a deep breath and thought, Massive overreaction, Libby.

She could feel his gaze but did not lift her head as she mumbled, 'I can manage.'

The frisson had passed but it had left her uncomfortably conscious of her own skin to the point where she could feel the individual hairs on the nape of her neck.

'We should—' she gave a heavy sigh of relief when her skirt came free '—play it safe.'

Rafael ran a hand across the stubble on his chin. *'We?'* he echoed, his attention drawn to the exposed nape of her neck. Rafael had never previously considered this part of a woman's anatomy sexually attractive.

'Good point,' she conceded with a cool smile that had earned her the name of ice maiden in her teens. 'However, you're the one bleeding.' And I'm the one who is getting a bad headache, she thought, conscious of the telltale pressure behind her eyes.

'You're tough, I get it, a regular man of steel and I'm impressed, believe me,' she continued, delivering a smile of brilliant insincerity. 'But watching someone bleed to death is not *my* style. Even someone as...' Libby registered the flash of stunned disbelief in his eyes and brought her tirade to an abrupt halt.

'Someone as?'

Libby shook her head, then gave a fractured gasp when without warning he reached out and casually took her chin between the long fingers of his right hand.

She was too startled by his action to resist as he tilted her face up to his. He was so close that she could see the gold tips on his sooty lashes and feel his warm breath on her face.

He moved a thumb in a lazy circular motion along the curve of her cheek and Libby's stomach went into dramatic free fall as every nerve ending in her body began to thrum.

Ignoring the small whisper of sanity in his head, he took her face between his hands and watched the brilliant blue of her sapphire eyes vanish as her pupils dilated rapidly.

He groaned something harsh on his own tongue as his eyes dropped to her lips.

'You're in pain!'

'How right you are.'

Libby struggled to fight her way out of the strange lethargy that crept over her; her limbs felt as though they didn't belong to her. 'Let me get help.' She started to pull away.

'You have a beautiful mouth.'

Libby stopped pulling as she thought, So do you.

He frowned suddenly. 'What is your name?'

Libby's throat was so dry her voice was barely above a whisper, barely audible above the pulsating thud of her heart as it tried to climb its way out of her chest. 'Libby.'

She'd read somewhere that head injuries could

make people act totally out of character—so what's *your* excuse, Libby?

'Libby?' He rolled the word around his tongue experimentally.

She nodded, hardly recognising her name when he said it, but finally placing his accent as Spanish.

'Look, this is silly—'

His mouth lowered, close but not quite touching, a whisper above her trembling lips.

What the hell are you doing, Rafael?

Rafael would have responded to the last-minute reassertion of sanity had she not at that exact moment given a choky little gasp and pressed her warm lips up against his.

A split second later with a scared little gasp she pulled back, but the damage was done.

Shame burned her cheeks as she met his eyes. 'That was so—'

'Not bad,' he inserted in a low sexy growl that did further serious damage to her already demolished nervous system. 'But I think we can do better.'

And he did.

His lips moved with slow sensuous skill across the trembling curve of her mouth; she heard herself whimper as he ran his tongue along the sensitive inner flesh of her lower lip and tugged the flesh gently between his teeth.

Libby, who had not moved a muscle, pulled back with a horrified gasp, breaking the connection before proceeding to fall out of the car in her haste to escape.

CHAPTER THREE

LIBBY stood there, hand pressed to her mouth as the horror of what she had just done hit home with the force of a hurricane.

This was one thing she could not blame on jet lag; she had lost control—sexually, with a stranger, a man whose name she didn't even know.

Mortified colour ebbed and flowed in her cheek. What had possessed her?

The answer to her question was getting out of what remained of the top-of-the-range sleek powerful car, his body language not suggestive of someone who had just survived a car smash or, for that matter, someone who had just kissed her passionately.

He looked… A soundless sigh escaped through her clenched teeth.

Shameful memories flashed through her mind.

For a breathless moment she could actually *feel* the texture of his lips, the taste of his hot mouth. Libby clenched her teeth, struggling to purge the image of his smouldering sexy eyes. She succeeded in pushing them away, but not before the hot core low in her pelvis had tightened to a hard fist of desire.

Knowing what she was feeling was shallow and only physical did not make the experience easier to cope with.

Her knees were shaking as, breath coming in a series of painful gasps, she watched covetously from under the sweep of her lashes as he stepped out onto the grass and stretched the kinks from his spine. The gorgeously cut suit was special and so was the tall Spaniard, and she wasn't just making excuses—he really was!

She swallowed. In the cramped confines of the car it had been obvious he was a powerfully built man, but until now she hadn't realised how dauntingly impressive his physique was.

Several inches over six feet, he had an athlete's body, greyhound lean and muscular, the width of his shoulders balanced by long legs—*very* long legs and narrow snaky hips.

As she continued to stare he walked around the car, inspecting the damage that would have made many men weep or at the very least swear, with an inscrutable expression on his lean patrician features. Libby felt her stomach flip.

She had never imagined that the way a man moved, even if it was with the grace and arrogance of a panther, would make her feel breathless.

Her unwilling appreciation gave way to indignation as he began to hit the keys on his phone. He hadn't even glanced her way!

She was shaking all over and he was acting as though nothing had happened, which on one level was good because the last thing she wanted right now was a post-mortem. She wanted to walk away, or possibly run, and forget it ever happened.

On the other level it *had* happened—he'd kissed her. Admittedly it wasn't a marriage proposal, but to act as though nothing had happened…well, it was just bad manners.

And she hated bad manners. It wasn't as if he'd turned her world upside down or anything dramatic and she'd stop shaking some time soon, but a show of penitence or even a thank you would have been something.

'What is the name of this place…?' he asked without looking up.

Libby glared with dislike at the top of his dark head. She could play it cool too. 'So you have a signal now?'

He deigned to notice her. 'Yes.' He angled an interrogative brow.

'Buckford,' Libby snapped.

'Buckford…?' Rafael repeated, wondering as he punched in the name why the name of a village in the middle of nowhere should sound vaguely familiar.

He returned to his text and Libby watched him, her temper rising. Jaw tight, she stomped up the hill.

Within seconds of sending the message Rafael received a text back from Gretchen, who assured him she would be with him in less than ten minutes. Satisfied with the response, he glanced up in time to see the redhead, whose progress up the muddy bank he'd been aware of in the periphery of his vision, bend over to slide one foot and then the other into a pair of heels.

The fresh air had cleared the remnants of haziness from his head and, sanity restored, Rafael was already regretting his impulsive actions. Struggling to control his temper, he recognised that his irritability was in part due to nothing more complicated than sexual frustration.

Regret or not, watching her shapely rear as she climbed the incline sent a stab of lust through his loins.

On the road above Libby stamped her feet, grimacing as her damp, muddy toes squelched inside her lovely new shoes. Anchoring her hair back from her face with one hand, she straightened up.

Even before she turned she knew he was watching her; she could *feel* his silent stare.

'What happened, that was unacceptable, even if you have got concussion,' she informed him icily.

'I do not have concussion.' Just an extremely

bad headache, but nothing a couple of aspirin would not cure. 'Though I am confused.'

A small choking sound left Libby's throat… *He's confused.*

'Are you implying that a man would need to have a head injury before he wants to kiss you?'

Thrown off her stride by the insert, Libby glared wrathfully at him. 'No, of course not. For your information a lot of men want to kiss me.'

His lips quivered. 'Of this I am sure.'

'If you do that again I'll…I'll…you'll be sorry!' Libby's hauteur suffered a wobble as she struggled against the impulse to turn and run as he began to stride up the steep incline, his progress a lot more sure-footed than her own had been.

He stepped onto the road and Libby immediately lost what height advantage geography had given her. He towered over her, forcing her to tilt her head to look him in the face. Size might not be everything but at that moment she would not have minded an extra inch or two.

'You kissed me,' she charged, addressing her accusation to his chest.

'Only after you kissed me.'

The provocation brought her indignant gaze zeroing in on his face. Libby thought longingly about wiping that smug smirk off his face. 'I'd had a shock. I thought you were dead.' As excuses went it was pathetic, but it was all she had.

'So that was the kiss of life?' he said, sounding interested.

Libby, who could not think of a smart comeback and suspected that even if she had he would have come up with an even smarter one, shook her head.

'I think we should forget it,' she decided magnanimously.

Libby intended to, though the incident had all the ingredients of a nightmare—the sort where you found yourself in the supermarket in your underwear, and not the good stuff.

'As you wish, though I'm insulted my kisses are so forgettable. Still, I'm a firm believer in the old adage practice makes perfect.'

Her eyes narrowed. Any more *perfect* and she'd

have passed out. 'So long as it's not with me you can practise as much as you like.'

'Relax, I only have sex with sane women.' Not for three months, he realized. This went a long way to explaining his uncharacteristically impulsive behaviour.

He had appetites, sure, but he exerted control and, he liked to think, discrimination. The last thing he wanted was to find himself involved with some needy attention seeking bunny boiler who wanted to *understand* him.

Luckily there were plenty of women who shared his pragmatic attitude to sex and did not need the façade of a *loving relationship* to enable them to enjoy sex.

Libby tilted her head back to angle a menacing frown at him. 'And you're saying I'm not?'

'You walked out in front of my car. If that doesn't qualify as insane I don't know what does.'

His eyes darkened at the memory of that moment when he had thought he was going to hit her. 'What did you think you were doing? I can't decide if you are a lunatic or just suicidal.'

The fact she fully deserved the reprimand and his anger did not make it easier to stand there meekly and take it.

'I didn't *jump out*, well, I did, but only because you were about to run over the dog and, anyway, if you hadn't been driving like an idiot this wouldn't have happened.'

He raised an eloquent brow. 'So this was my fault.'

Libby felt the guilty heat rush to her cheeks. 'Not totally,' she admitted reluctantly.

'And as for a dog...' he made a show of looking around before lifting his shoulders in an expressive shrug '...I see no dog.'

The pink in her cheeks deepened to an angry red. 'Are you calling me a liar?' she asked in a dangerous tone.

He arched a brow and looked amused. 'I am simply saying that I saw no dog...' He turned his head from one side to the other and shrugged. 'I *see* no dog.'

'Just because you don't see something doesn't mean it wasn't there!' retorted Libby, really angry now. Did he really think the dog was a figment of her imagination?

'Let's for argument's sake say there *was* a dog—'

Libby gritted her teeth. 'There *was* a dog. He's a golden Lab who answers to the name of Eustace.'

Libby saw no reason to add that he rarely answered to his name. In fact the daft animal was far more likely to run in the opposite direction.

'So where is this dog now?'

Good question, thought Libby, scanning the lane with a worried frown. 'God knows,' she admitted honestly. 'He's not very… He was a rescue dog—he's a little bit…highly strung.' It sounded better than the truth, which was he was as mad as a box of frogs!

'If a dog is badly behaved it is the owner's fault and not the animal's.'

Libby, her chin angled defiantly, tilted her head back to meet his golden stare. His superior attitude was really setting her teeth on edge.

'I'm not blaming the dog for anything and I am

quite prepared to admit that the accident is my fault,' she told him haughtily.

He shook his head and flashed a wolfish white grin. 'Has no one ever told you that you should never admit guilt?'

Libby gave a disdainful sniff and retorted, 'No, I was taught to tell the truth and take responsibility for my own actions.'

'Very noble, I'm impressed,' he said, looking deeply unimpressed. 'Not everyone realises that all actions have consequences.'

Libby regarded him warily.

'In the litigious world of today such painful honesty can be an expensive luxury.'

Libby shivered and, hugging herself, rubbed at the goose bumps that had broken out on her arms. Some women, she was sure, would have found the resulting suggestion of something approaching cruelty in his smile attractive; she was glad she was not one of them.

But, God, he knew how to kiss!

'Is that some sort of threat?'

Before he could reply the sound of an excitedly

barking dog bursting through the bushes the other side of the road made them both turn.

'Is he real enough for you?' Libby raised a sarcastic brow and threw him a challenging glare of triumph as she dropped gracefully down to dog level.

'Eustace, good boy!'

The dog continued to bark from an elusive distance.

Rafael watched her efforts to lure him closer with a critical scowl. 'At heart a dog is still a wolf, a pack animal who needs to know who is in charge.'

Libby cast him a sideways look of dislike as she continued to make encouraging noises. 'And that I suppose would be you.' Admittedly if any man had pack alpha written all over him it was this one.

'My lifestyle is not conducive to owning pets.' That was the life he had chosen for himself, the life that suited him. No baggage, nobody to feel responsible for.

He had given responsibility a go and he had

failed; the guilt of failing the person he had tried to protect had stayed with him through the years.

He had failed the only person he had ever loved.

It didn't matter to Rafael that most people would have considered it the mother's job to keep the son safe and not vice versa. His mother had been one of life's fragile souls worn down by rejection and hungry for the approval of whatever man was in her life, eager to gain their approval even when pleasing them meant dumping her inconvenient child with whoever would take him.

She had always come back for him eaten up with guilt, calling him the only man in her life, and for a while things were good, but there was always another man. And then finally she had not come back and Rafael had gone in search of her, arriving too late.

She had died alone in a remote village that did not even have clean water, let alone a doctor, and Rafael had not been able to afford a headstone.

He had been fifteen at the time and it had taken him two years to return with a headstone. The village now had clean running water and last year he had laid the foundation stone of a clinic.

'But that doesn't stop you being an expert,' Libby drawled. 'Why aren't I surprised? For your information Eustace was badly abused. He needs TLC, not bullying and he—' Just warming to her theme, Libby suddenly stopped as the tension he was vibrating reached her. She tilted her head back to look at his face.

'Are you all right?'

She was confused as much by her reaction to the shocking desolation she had glimpsed in his heavy-lidded eyes as by the cause of it, and her questioning gaze went to a possible source: his head wound.

'Your head?' Not that physical pain would explain the awful anguish she had glimpsed in his eyes.

Rafael looked into her wide eyes, blue as a summer sky and warm with concern, and fought the illogical impulse to lash out, punish her for seeing more than she was meant to.

'My head is fine,' he said, taking a step forward

while mentally taking several backwards, pushing away the dark memories and focusing instead on the pleasant present and the more than pleasant tantalising glimpse of cleavage revealed as he stared down the neck of her loose necked sweater.

'So you understand about animals.'

Catching the direction of his bold stare, Libby felt her breasts tingle. And for a moment there she had been in danger of imagining he had some depth! She gave a disgusted snort and swung away. The fact her body continued to react without her consent increased her self-disgust.

'Let's put it this way—I find them infinitely preferable to men,' she gritted, feeling impelled to add, 'Some men.' She pretended not to hear his husky laugh. 'So if you don't mind.' She turned back to him and mimed a zipping motion across her lips.

After a startled moment Rafael grinned and inclined his dark head. 'Be my guest.'

Libby, aware of her silent critic, continued her attempt to coax Eustace to her until her patience snapped. She rose to her feet, muttering under her breath as she dragged a swathe of hair back from her face before directing a frustrated glare his way.

'Fine, if you're so clever…?' she snapped, irrationally hoping he was equally unsuccessful.

Of course he wasn't.

He stepped forward, said a couple of authoritative-sounding words in his own language, and the dog—suddenly he could speak Spanish—trotted forward meekly looking sheepish.

Libby gritted her teeth and thought, Traitor, as after another word the dog sat down at his feet, wagging his tail while he gazed adoringly up at the man who condescended to pat his head and murmur a word of praise before bending to gather the lead from the ground.

Libby's chest swelled with indignation, making her even more uncomfortably conscious of the fabric chafing against her nipples. It was a conspiracy, she brooded darkly, first betrayed by her own body and now the dog.

Libby took the lead silently proffered her and viewed him through narrowed eyes. 'If I took you home my family would probably want to adopt you.' She drew the dog towards her, patting his head.

'Would that not make me your brother?' he taunted.

'I already have a brother, and I'm sure you have your own family.' And maybe a wife?

The possibility filled her with horror. Had she kissed not just a stranger, but a *married* stranger? Checking out his left hand, she was relieved to see no wedding band.

Rafael shook his head. 'No, my mother died some years ago. There is no one else of note.'

'That is so sad!' Libby exclaimed.

CHAPTER FOUR

'SAD?' Rafael raised a brow and watched the glow of sympathy fade from her blue eyes as he added cynically, 'From what I see of families I am not envious. Down,' he added in a stern aside as the dog, whimpering, rubbed against his leg.

The dog immediately rolled onto his back submissively.

'Eustace!' Exasperated, Libby tugged the dog back towards her. 'You really are an idiot!'

'I have been called worse.'

'Not you…' Libby saw the mocking glint in his deep-set eyes and, fighting a grin, added gruffly, 'Well, you are, but on this occasion I was talking to the dog.'

Rafael's mouth twisted into a sardonic smile that faded as a car came round the corner.

Libby, aware that she had lost his attention,

turned in the direction of his gaze and saw a bright red classic sports car driven with the top down heading towards them at a sedate pace.

The driver waved when she spotted them and slowed.

Rafael did not wave, but it seemed a safe bet to Libby that the woman who parked the car and leapt gracefully from the vehicle was not a stranger.

Libby watched the woman's progress, envying the voluptuous figure, the length of her legs and her ability to make skin-tight jeans look good. From a distance she looked fantastic, depressingly close to she looked even more perfect.

Libby watched the woman's fashionable twenties bob swinging in a silky bell around her face and envied the sleekness of a style she could never achieve with her own naturally curly hair.

'Ra— Oh, God, *blood*!' exclaimed the blonde, clapping a hand to her mouth. 'I feel sick.'

So did Libby. What sort of man kissed another woman while his girlfriend was on her way to rescue him?

'Kindly endeavour not to be sick.'

She had her answer: the sort of man who spoke to his girlfriend like that, Libby thought, wondering why the woman not only took the harsh advice in her stride, but appeared *grateful*!

'Sorry I'm late. I got stuck behind a tractor. Do you think it will scar?' she wondered, her eyes trained with sick fascination on his injured face. 'Have you cleaned it? There could be dirt.'

Sensing that his PA was about to go into full OCD mode, Rafael pitched his reply in a tone aimed at defusing the situation before it got out of hand.

When she had a handle on her compulsive behaviour Gretchen was the best PA he had ever had, but when she lost it things could get...interesting. Like the time the cleaning supervisor had rung him at midnight saying he might want to know that his assistant was still there switching the light on and off, unable to leave the room.

In retrospect he could see that the clues that should have alerted him to her condition had been there, he just hadn't noticed. This did not make

Rafael feel good about himself. He expected those who worked for him to go the extra mile and what he expected he should also be prepared to give. One of the first lessons Rafael had learnt was that loyalty was a two-way street.

He had refused to accept her tearfully offered resignation, pointing out that it made no sense to lose the best PA he had ever had just because she felt the need to spend an hour washing her hands.

Instead he had acquired the name of a clinical psychologist who came highly recommended and insisted that she undertake therapy sessions. It had been a good call—they had proved dramatically successful but, as Gretchen said herself, she was a work in progress.

'The wound has been cleaned,' Rafael said, pre-empting the production of the cleaning products he knew would be in her car.

Libby opened her mouth to indignantly refute this and found herself on the receiving end of a killer look. She gave as good as she got glarewise and lapsed into tight-lipped silence.

'And you are not late.'

Gretchen shook her head and glanced fretfully at her watch. 'I said ten minutes and it's—'

Rafael cut her off. 'You are here now.'

'Yes, I am.' She flashed her boss a smile and took a deep breath. 'Thanks. I've arranged a tow truck and rung ahead to delay the meeting with the Russians and—' She stopped and let out a yelp as the Labrador laid a friendly muddy paw on her leg.

Rafael clicked his tongue in irritation. 'Down!' The disapproving look that went with the command was aimed at Libby, not the dog. 'Can you not control that animal?'

'Not according to you,' Libby flashed.

A few feet away the tall gorgeous blonde continued to pat frantically at her jeans, making what seemed to Libby like an awful lot of fuss over a tiny amount of mud. The woman had barely glanced her way, let alone introduced herself. They were suited in more ways than one, both beautiful and both incredibly rude, then it hit her—she didn't even know his name!

'It is nothing, Gretchen, relax.'

The blonde looked at the hand on her shoulder and gave a gulping gasp, then with one last fretful dab at the invisible speck of dirt lifted her head. 'I really don't like the country.'

'Wait for me in the car.'

And she did.

His ability to inspire unquestioning obedience was obviously not restricted to the canine community, it worked on beautiful six-foot blondes as well.

'Does everyone jump when you snap your fingers?' Libby screwed up her nose and gave a pained grimace. 'I said that out loud, didn't I?'

Rafael nodded, his lips twitching. 'The answer to your question is no.' The redhead did not jump except in the opposite direction—perhaps that was the attraction…? On the other hand it might be the incredible body and the lush lips.

Libby did not need to pretend surprise. 'You amaze me.'

'I have that effect.'

Libby's stomach took a sharp unscheduled dip as the explicit glow in his expressive eyes sent a rush of shameful heat through her body. Molten hot, it settled disturbingly between her thighs.

Libby flushed, her anger at least in part aimed at the weakness that made her respond to him this way.

'I'm not interested. Maybe you should try and *amaze* your girlfriend.'

His brows lifted as he encountered the hostility shining in her eyes. 'Gretchen is my PA, not my girlfriend, and I do not mix business with pleasure.' He stopped, an arrested look filtering into his eyes as he realised he had just broken the habit of a lifetime and explained himself.

Libby gave an airy shrug to establish she had no interest in his relationship with the blonde whatsoever. The knowing gleam in his heavy-lidded eyes suggested she wasn't entirely convincing.

'You shouldn't keep your…' she jerked her head towards the red car '…*PA* waiting.'

He directed a frowning glance towards the car; she was right. 'True.'

'Don't let me keep you.' The words were barely

out of her mouth before she gave a contradictory urgent cry of, 'Wait!'

'You are missing me already. I'm touched.'

Libby directed an 'if I see you again in this lifetime it will be too soon' look at him and pulled a scrap of paper from her pocket. 'Do you have a pen?'

Rafael pulled a pen from his jacket pocket and watched as she began to scribble on the paper.

'Here,' Libby said, pushing it at him.

'What is this—your telephone number?'

'My name and address,' she retorted, refusing to react to the mockery in his voice. She glanced towards the damaged vehicle. 'Send me the bill for the damage.'

Rafael glanced down at the words on the paper. 'That could be quite a bill.'

'I pay my debts,' she told him proudly. 'Is something wrong?' she asked, frowning as he did a visible double take.

'Marchant? Would that connect you to Marchant Plastics?'

'My grandfather began the firm and my dad

runs it now. Have I said something amusing?' she asked spikily. 'What are you doing?' she added as he screwed up the paper between his long fingers. 'I mean it—I want to pay for the damage.'

'I won't hold you to it, but don't worry, I have an excellent memory.'

Puzzling over the cryptic parting shot, Libby stood watching as he walked away and got into the car with the beautiful blonde, not once looking back.

Of course he didn't look back! He had probably already dismissed her from his memory, or maybe he was sharing an amusing anecdote about the incident with his blonde PA—sure, that was *really* likely.

Eustace sat on the passenger seat with his head out of the window as Libby drove the half-mile down the lane to the chocolate-box roses-around-the-door cottage where Chloe lived.

The short journey did not take long, though longer than it might have had she not felt the need to stop halfway to bury her head in her hands and groan a mortified— You wanted to kiss him; you *enjoyed* it!

It seemed to Libby as she angled a glance at her refection in the driving mirror that her shame was written all over her face. Chloe was going to know that something had happened the moment she saw her and in her present frame of mind Libby had an uncomfortable feeling she might tell her what it was!

Hand on the ignition key, she paused and dropped her hand, thinking, Maybe not…? It might be an invitation to any passing felon, but a running engine also provided an escape route of the 'must dash, the engine's running' variety. And Chloe was already aware that she was in a hurry home.

Her precautions proved unnecessary as it was Chloe's husband, Joe, who answered the door. Not really renowned for his sartorial elegance, Joe resembled an unmade bed even more so than normal and the bags under his eyes had acquired company.

Libby's own problems receded momentarily as

she angled a look of sympathy at his exhausted face. 'Hi, Joe.'

Beside her Eustace saw his master and leapt at him, tearing the lead from her hand in the process.

'Hush, you'll wake the baby, hound,' Joe said, grabbing the trailing lead of the barking dog and receiving a slobbery kiss from the overexcited animal before bestowing a grateful but weary smile on Libby. 'Thanks, Libby. It turns out I could have picked him up—I got off work early.'

Now he tells me, Libby thought, fixing a smile. 'No problem.'

Other than discovering I am actually not a *nice* girl. That actually when it comes to breathtakingly handsome Spaniards I am what is termed *easy*.

On the plus side, it was good to know your weaknesses. From now on she was going to avoid anywhere where there was so much as a chance of hearing flamenco music.

'The vet said you can bring him back Tuesday to get the stitches out and to give him these.' She reached into her pocket and produced a bottle of tablets. 'Twice a day, I think he said,' she said, glancing at the label.

Joe took them and pocketed them. 'Don't worry, we know the drill—unfortunately.' Joe ran a hand over his unshaven jaw and seemed surprised to find gingery stubble there. 'But no more or it's obedience school for you,' he warned, patting the animal's head.

Libby fought back a smile. Poor Joe—designer stubble was not a good look on him. Of course there were some men who would not necessarily look disagreeable with a couple of days' beard growth.

A few might even look sexy in a slightly edgy, piratical way, she conceded, thinking of one face in particular.

'How are things?' she asked, making a conscious and unsuccessful effort to push the face away.

'A bit…twilight zone, really. I think it's the sleep deprivation. Chloe's having a nap. I know she'd love to see you, but you don't mind if I don't wake her…?'

Finally banishing the image of a specific dark lean face complete with designer stubble, Libby shook her head and struggled to hide her relief.

'Not a problem. To be honest I'm a bit tired. I want to get home and Mum and Dad—'

'Yes, of course!' A spasm of sympathy crossed Joe's face. 'I heard, Libby. I'm *so* sorry. If there is any—' He broke off, looking over his shoulder and groaning as the unmistakeable sound of a baby's demanding cry rang out in the distance.

Oblivious to the alarm in Libby's expression, he gave an apologetic shrug. 'Sorry, must go before Chloe wakes up. She's all in and—'

'No problem, you go and give my love to Ch—'

'You're a pal.'

If Libby had not stepped back the door might have hit her nose. As it was she turned her ankle on the cobbles that ran around the house.

Teeth gritted and ignoring the stabbing sharp pain in her ankle, she retraced her steps, the sound of Joe's voice amplified in her head above the sound of her feet on the gravel driveway—*I heard, I'm so sorry...*

Heard what? Sorry about what?

She had to fight the impulse to run back to the cottage, bang on the door and demand that Joe explain himself. However the sound of the dog barking and the baby crying did suggest that Joe had enough on his plate…and anyway she might be misreading what he had said.

She shook her head. Deep down she knew this wasn't the case. She wasn't misreading anything or overreacting—she had *known* something was wrong!

And how did she respond to a potential family crisis? She stopped off to kiss a total stranger on her way home!

The fact the kissing had not been planned did not constitute an excuse in Libby's mind. It did make it all the more difficult for her to forgive herself for her reprehensible behaviour.

Resisting the impulse to floor the accelerator—she'd already caused one accident today—Libby drove through the village at a sedate pace responding mechanically to the waves she received from several people. Was she being paranoid or had there been sympathy in those waves? It was a small community and everyone pretty much knew everyone—and secrets, forget it, there weren't any.

She was probably the only person in a twenty-mile radius who wasn't in the know, Libby thought as she struggled to keep her imagination in check.

She failed miserably. By the time she slowed automatically to negotiate a particularly awkward hairpin bend a mile beyond the village her fertile imagination had gone into overdrive to the point where she felt physically sick.

'Please let everything be all right.'

Just two hundred yards further was the driveway for Maple House. People who did not know the area frequently missed the turn and drove past. Hardly surprising—it had once been an impressive entrance but, like the house it led to, had seen better days. One weathered stone griffon had fallen off his sentinel perch on the high, once-ornate but now crumbling gatepost. One of the massive wrought-iron gates that had once borne the name of her family home lay propped up against the wall—reattaching it was one of those tasks that somehow no one had got around to—covered by ivy and moss.

Libby did not notice the signs of decay and neglect that might strike a stranger as, her white face set in a pale mask of apprehension, she drove down the potholed tree-lined driveway with scant regard for the suspension of the car she drove.

The sight of the people carrier her brother and his wife had traded their smart sports car in for after the birth of their twin sons two years ago did not encourage optimism.

It was definitely not a good sign. She was glad her brother was here, but she knew that with the imminence of her due date and the problems heavily pregnant Meg had had with her blood pressure during this pregnancy he wouldn't have left her alone with the twins and made the long trip down from Scotland for anything that wasn't urgent.

After being away the first sight of the mellow stone of the façade of her home usually gave Libby a sense of calm and well-being. No matter what problems she had the old stone walls had always represented safety and security and a sense of continuity. Those feelings were absent as she stepped out on the gravelled driveway.

The silence barring the song of the wood pigeons was another ominous sign. The Marchants, not a family renowned for their reserve, did noisy welcomes, and normally they would have been crowding around her before she had been able to open the car door, acting as though she'd been away for a year rather than few weeks, all talking at once and queuing to hug her.

Where were they?

Unease crept like a cold bony finger up her spine as she marched across the noisy gravel to the stone steps that led to the big front door, Libby still half expecting it to open and her family to spill out.

It didn't. With a shaking hand she fished her key from her handbag and opened it. The only sound in the panelled hallway she entered was the ticking of the grandfather clock that kept erratic time.

'Mum! Dad! Ed...?' she called as she bent to

pick up the pile of mail, mostly circulars, from the doormat and kicked the door shut with her foot. As she did so the drawing-room door swung open and her sister-in-law, a heavily pregnant pretty brunette—even when her sunny face was creased into a dark frown—appeared.

'Meg?' Libby blinked, startled. A five-hundred-mile journey with two-year-old twins did not by any stretch of the imagination constitute rest, which was what Libby knew the doctors had prescribed for her sister-in-law. 'What are you doing here?'

'Libby, oh, God, am I glad to see you! It's terrible, I don't know what to do and Ed is so...' Meg stopped, shaking her head and biting her lip.

Libby caught her arm. So far reality was proving more alarming than the worst of her nightmare imaginings. 'What's wrong, Meg?' Amazingly her voice sounded calm and steady.

The older woman caught her trembling lower lip between her teeth. 'Everything!' she wailed.

This came from a woman who she had once seen deliver a sharp reprimand to a would-be mugger.

Libby sucked in a deep breath and straightened her shoulders. It was dawning on her that the reality of this situation might actually be as bad as the worst of her imaginings.

The knot of dread in her stomach tightened as Libby limped past her weeping sister-in-law into the drawing room.

Nobody spoke when she entered. The bone-deep chill that hit her had nothing to do with the fact there was no cheerful fire burning in the ornate marble fireplace.

A pall of gloom hung in the air so heavy it seemed to suck in the light from the room. Despite this Libby's first reaction was actually relief—everyone was alive!

'Thank God!' she breathed.

The comment earned her a look of incredulity from her grim-faced elder brother, a blank stare from her father—her mum rather bizarrely continued to trim the ends off the roses she was placing in a large arrangement on the bureau, the contrast of the normality of her actions adding to the surreal quality of the scene. Libby wasn't sure if she had even registered her presence.

'Is anyone going to tell me what's wrong?'

For a moment it seemed as though no one was, then her father stood up slowly. He might not have suffered a heart attack but he looked as though it might happen any moment.

Watching him, Libby thought, He's old, Dad's old. The thought shocked her. She had never thought of her father that way before, even after his heart attack.

'Aldo Alejandro is dead.'

A frown formed between Libby's feathery brows. The name triggered a vague image of a large man who had lifted her off her feet and swung her high in the air—he had seemed to take her squeals of terror as squeals of delight.

'That's sad.' Sad, but it did not explain the air of impending doom. 'Sorry, Dad, you were close?' Not close enough surely to even partly explain the grey tinge in her father's normally ruddy complexion.

'He was always a good friend to me.' Her father's voice broke and Libby watched with horror as tears began to slide down his cheeks.

Her brother moved away from his sentinel position by the window and strode over to his father's side. 'The grandson has inherited and he's calling in the loan.'

Libby blinked, confused. 'What loan?'

Philip Marchant cleared his throat. 'We'd been having a few cash-flow problems—when the bank wouldn't let me take a second mortgage out on the house Aldo helped me out with a loan.'

Second mortgage? Libby hadn't even known there was a first mortgage. She turned to her brother. 'Did you know?'

He nodded.

'So what does this mean?' Libby asked, dividing the question between her brother and father.

Behind her Meg said, 'I must check on the boys.' And fled the room.

'I shouldn't have let her come with me,' Ed said as he followed her from the room.

Libby kept her eyes trained on her father's face. 'What does it mean, Dad?'

'It means that we are going to lose the firm and the house—I'll be bankrupt.'

'This house!' Libby shook her head, looking around the room filled with a lifetime of memories. 'No, that can't be right. How is it possible? You have to speak to the grandson, explain that people rely on you, that—'

Kate Marchant stopped rearranging the flowers crammed in the big vase on the bureau and turned to face her daughter. 'Sit down, Libby, and shut up!' The yellow rose in her hand fell to the floor as her daughter and husband stared at her in varying degrees of astonishment.

Libby responded to the uncharacteristic abrupt directive without thinking. Sinking into the chintz chair she struggled to recall the last time she had heard her mother raise her voice, let alone speak harshly to her.

'This is hard enough for your father to explain without you interrupting. Do you really think he would be telling you this now if he hadn't already tried everything else?'

Libby swallowed. 'But what will happen to the

staff? Doesn't this man know that they'll lose their jobs, that their expertise will be lost? Doesn't he care?'

'Of course he doesn't care,' her mother returned bitterly. 'The man is a total monster!'

Philip Marchant walked over to his wife and pulled her into his arms. 'I had a meeting with him yesterday, Libby, and I'm afraid there is no chance of him changing his mind.'

'So what are we going to do?' Libby asked, feeling oddly numb as she listened to the sound of her mother's heart-wrenching sobs. *Mum doesn't cry.*

Philip shrugged. 'Nothing,' he said wearily. 'It's out of our hands now.'

Libby shook her head, frustrated by this defeatist attitude. Nothing was impossible; they had to fight. 'But maybe if we spoke to the bank—'

Libby broke off as her brother ran into the room, an expression of fear and panic on his face that would stay with her for ever.

'Come quick, it's Meg—the baby is coming!'

CHAPTER FIVE

RAFAEL ALEJANDRO'S strongly delineated dark brows drew together in a dark line above his hawklike nose as the raised voices emanating from the outer office made him break off for the second time.

'This is ridiculous!' His tone irritable, he unfolded his long lean length from his seat and strode purposefully towards the door, pausing to offer a curt word of apology to the man who was seated at the other side of the big desk.

Rafael had no problem with Gretchen scheduling her therapy session during office hours, but he had a big problem with the woman she had arranged to stand in for the couple of hours she was away from her desk.

Last week her useless substitute had not relayed an important message, this week she was taking part in what sounded like some sort of catfight!

'No problem,' Max Croft said with an easy-going shrug. 'Someone doesn't sound very happy,' he added half to himself as Rafael, his chiselled features set in a dark scowl, wrenched the door open.

The female voices got louder and the older man felt a passing flicker of sympathy for the unknown person or persons responsible for putting the scowl on Rafael Alejandro's face. There was a very good reason why people avoided inviting the Spaniard's displeasure.

Rafael had earned his reputation—possibly exaggerated, but Max, a prudent man, was not about to put it to the test—as a person who did not suffer fools gladly and who suffered people who crossed him not at all.

His wealth and power made him a man that people automatically wanted to please, but Max suspected that even without the wealth he was a man that people would have trodden lightly around. The fact that nobody actually knew how he had amassed his great wealth, though there were many theories, only added to the mystique that had developed around the man.

There was dynamic and then there was, he mused, Rafael Alejandro, who was to his mind more a force of nature!

About to walk into the room adjoining, Rafael paused, head tilted a little to one side as he identified one of the angry voices. The exquisite little face that matched the husky voice flashed into his head, and the resulting blast of neat testosterone that flooded into his bloodstream made his mind grow blank.

It took him a couple of seconds to regain control of his mental faculties. Abandoning the effort to effect similar control over his body—Rafael recognised a lost cause when he felt one—he began sifting possible explanations for this unexpected visit as he turned back to the other man.

'Max, would you mind if we finished off the details next week? Something has come up.'

'No problem,' Max replied, curious but careful not to show it.

As the other man got to his feet Rafael walked

away from the doorway and crossed the room, where he opened the fire door.

'I'll be in touch,' he promised.

Impressively the other man walked past him acting as if he got asked to leave via the fire exit every day of the week.

Rafael closed the door and nodded his approval. In his experience more important than knowing when to ask a question was knowing when *not* to ask a question.

The question, Rafael asked himself as he stood a silent observer to the events unfolding in his outer office, was why?

Why was Libby Marchant here?

He did not have the faintest idea but he now knew why he paid Gretchen her outrageously high salary—she earned it and then some. On her watch this farcical scene would never have occurred.

Unobserved he watched Gretchen's pink-cheeked and harassed stand-in angle a look of narrow-eyed dislike at the young woman sitting on the floor in the middle of the room.

'I am sorry, Ms Marchant, that you have had a wasted journey, but as I have already explained—'

'I don't need your apology or your explanations.'

'What do you need?'

At the sound of his voice both women spun around to face him.

Rafael scanned the face turned up to him, eyes a deep cobalt blue that blazed back at him, no tears, just ferocious contempt and anger reflected in the sparkling surface as she blinked once, then blinked again.

He saw recognition then shock register in her eyes a split second before her lips parted to release a fractured gasp of horror.

The soft sound drew his gaze to that lovely lush softness of her mouth. He felt his body harden in helpless response to the images floating through his mind. Images that portrayed those lips moving across his skin, over his body.

'You…?' Fighting her way through what felt like layers of fuzzy cotton wool in her brain, Libby

shook her head to clear the fog. 'I don't understand…'

She would, and when she did he imagined there
would be some interesting and possibly noisy fire-
works. Rafael resigned himself to the inevitability
of it.

'What *do* you need, *querida*?' he repeated his
question.

She didn't answer and he found himself thinking of what he needed.

He needed a lot.

He needed everything.

He stood for a moment, literally frozen to the
spot by a tide of primal lust that washed over him,
lust so primitive and potent that for the space of
several heartbeats it wiped everything else from
his head.

Clawing his way slowly above the shimmering
primal blur dancing across his vision, he raked a
not quite steady hand through his dark hair, struggling to rationalise the primitive strength of his
reaction to this woman's beauty.

Life was not going to return to normal until he

did something about this situation, he decided, thinking along the lines of a short-term, passionate affair. Of course the Marchant connection complicated the situation, but the problem was not insuperable.

While the thoughts were running through his head, somewhere in the periphery of his vision Rafael was conscious of the stand-in, whose name at that moment totally eluded him—hard to think names when you were thinking of being inside the warm heat of a woman's body—stepping out from behind her desk to join him.

She remained utterly oblivious to the fact that her presence was surplus to requirements—he might actually give Gretchen a raise—as she directed an accusing glare towards Libby Marchant.

'This person—' she stabbed an accusing finger at Libby '—I asked her to leave, I said—'

'You said he was not in the building.' Feeling as if she were living a nightmare, Libby turned her attention from the woman back to the man standing there. She shook her head.

'Are you here to see Rafael Alejandro too?' Unlikely but not impossible and definitely preferable to the other explanation—the one she couldn't even bring herself to acknowledge.

The slight negative shake of his dark head drew a sharp little gasp from her throat.

'I came here to see Rafael Alejandro. Are *you* Rafael Alejandro?'

He tipped his dark head in acknowledgement. 'I am.'

Libby's hand went to her mouth as she closed her eyes, remembering the moments the previous night when she had sat in the hospital watching the people she loved most in the world unhappy and in pain, able to do nothing but fetch coffee from the vending machine that nobody drank, then fetch some more when it got cold.

Escaping for a short time into her own private fantasy world had not seemed so terrible, and if thinking about a man's face, allowing the memory of his lips, his taste, the hard virile strength of his body to fill her mind and block out the nightmare for a short time meant she was able to stay strong for her family and offer the support they needed it, had seemed defensible.

Defensible…!

A violent wave of shame and revulsion washed over her. The man she had fantasised about was the reason they were there; he was the reason why Meg and Ed's tiny baby was in an incubator unable to breathe without the aid of machines.

She opened her eyes and admitted to herself, This man, that face—and hated herself.

She hated him.

Rafael watched the expressions flicker across her face before finally settling into contemptuous fury.

'You knew who I was yesterday?' Of course he did. Libby swallowed the bubble of hysteria lodged in her aching throat. 'You are a despicable man!'

He angled a sardonic brow. 'A little harsh.'

'A little harsh?' she echoed. 'You ruined my father.'

A spasm of irritation tugged at the corners of his mouth. '*I* did not ruin your father. Your father—'

He broke off, shaking his head. 'It is not relevant—that was business.'

'Business?' she said, looking at him incredulously. 'It feels pretty personal to me!'

The stand-in turned to Rafael, her expression apologetic. 'I asked her to leave and she became abusive.'

Libby's brows rose in indignation. 'If you think that was abuse you've led a very sheltered life!'

'I've called Security, sir. I told her and she just sat down. I think she's a bit...' a wary eye on Libby, the woman tapped her head significantly '...not quite right.'

Rafael's eyes did not leave Libby's face as he rapped back flatly, 'Then uncall them.'

The woman's mouth fell open. 'But...'

Rafael looked her way and arched a brow. The woman blenched and starting nodding. but Rafael was already walking across to where Libby was still sitting.

'The sit-in is quite unnecessary,' he said, stretching out a hand towards her.

Libby looked at his hand, gave a contemptuous snort and got to her feet unaided.

Hands on her hips, she tilted her head back to direct a challenging stare at his face. The silence stretched as her eyes were drawn to the strips stretched neatly across the wound on his head; the white plaster stood out against his olive-toned skin.

'Yes, it is painful if that makes you feel better.'

'It does,' she admitted, thinking, You do not know the meaning of pain.

Pain was what she had seen in the eyes of her brother as he kept vigil by his baby daughter's cot. 'Do you know where I have just come from?'

'Why don't you tell me, as you are clearly aching to do so?'

'The hospital.' At least that wiped the smug smirk off his face. 'Because of you my sister-in-law went into premature labour. If anything happens to her or her baby it will be down to you! And if it does,' she promised, eyeing him with contempt, 'I will make you wish you had never been born.'

Rafael took on board the information but did not react to the threat; instead he studied her.

Yesterday's mud-stained fashionable outfit was gone, replaced by a pair of jeans that clung to the slim curves of her thighs. It was topped by a cashmere sweater a shade paler than her incredible eyes.

With no make-up, she looked as though she had just stepped straight from a shower with her still damp wildly curling hair hanging loose around her clean-scrubbed pale face.

She looked so young he suddenly felt old and jaded by comparison.

She also looked dead on her feet and perilously close to collapse. Not happy to identify the emotion that tightened his chest as concern, he barked, 'What in the name of God were your family doing letting you come here in this state?'

This pretence of concern enraged her further. 'My family...my family are devastated. My father is a broken man. Imagine how he feels right now!'

Rafael tried and failed. He had never had family support to fall back on, just his own wits. How would it feel to be part of a family that was ready to do battle on his behalf?

His glance drifted over her angry face.

Or at least one member was.

Rafael didn't have a clue, but he suspected that there would be many who, broke or not, would envy Philip Marchant.

He did not include himself in this number.

'Did you know he only had a heart attack last year? Did you know he had a *triple* bypass?' she demanded, her voice quavering at the memory of walking into his study and finding her dad lying on the floor clutching his chest.

She would never forget the sheer terror and utter helplessness she had felt as she'd held his cold, clammy hand and waited for the ambulance to arrive. The minutes had felt like hours. She still relived them regularly in her nightmares.

'No, I did not know.'

Her blue eyes darkened with distaste as they came to rest on his face. 'It wouldn't have made any difference, would it?' she charged contemptuously. 'You don't give a damn who you hurt.'

The exhaustion that was creeping over her slurred her words as she yelled, 'My brother is still at the hospital.'

'Is the baby very premature?'

'I'm not going to discuss my family with you!' she raged.

'I thought that was what you were doing,' he observed before turning to the hovering stand-in who was eating up every word. 'When Gretchen gets back tell her to cancel my appointments for this afternoon.'

'Come.' He slung an impatient look Libby's way. 'You need to sit down.' He gestured towards his office door.

She shook her head mulishly. 'I was sitting down. You made me get up.'

'Let me rephrase that—you can walk under your own steam or I will carry you.'

She looked at him in horror. 'You wouldn't dare.'

'Wrong reply,' he said, casually swinging her into his arms.

She responded with kicks interspersed with squeals of outrage.

'You remind me of a piglet I used to know,' he said, placing her back on her feet in the middle of his office. 'I'd say take a seat but I'm afraid that might trigger another act of civil disobedience. You know, you really should have called the press if you wanted to exploit the situation to the full.'

Libby stood there breathing hard. 'How dare you manhandle me? And how do you know I haven't called the press?' she challenged.

'Have you?'

'I called the local news station,' she lied inventively as she made a great show of consulting her watch. 'I'd say they should be arriving just about—now.' She lifted her head and smiled. 'They'll love seeing a crying woman ejected by your bully boys.'

'Never play poker—you'd lose.' Rafael scanned the face turned up to him; the eyes, a deep cobalt blue, that blazed back at him were dry.

'You're not crying,' he pointed out mildly.

'I will be,' she promised grimly, and then, just

in case he didn't believe her, she produced her party trick. Allowing her eyes to fill with tears, she blinked to allow one to escape the shimmering depths before wiping it away with the back of her hand and angling a challenging stare up at the tall man who had casually brought ruin to her family.

How many other families had he casually ruined? He didn't care—men like him were geared to achieving a goal and to hell with whom they hurt in the process.

She sat down in the chair that was pushed behind her, just managing to bite back the polite thank you—good manners were as hard to break as bad habits and frequently much more inconvenient.

Not as inconvenient as her weird physical response to this man.

It wasn't just the fact he was very easy on the eye, the most beautiful man she had ever seen or even imagined. She could not have reacted more strongly if she had turned her head and seen a jungle cat standing in the air-conditioned office.

Or is it just me? Libby pushed away the half-formed thought.

His dark brows sketched upwards in mock admiration. 'An impressive trick with the tears, although one you can only employ once.' Far from being moved by women's tears, he usually reacted to such displays of emotion with irritation.

Ironically it was her bogus tears that had got to him.

'It always worked with my brother.' The reminder of Ed brought a fresh rush of tears to her eyes, this time for real. Her shoulders slumped as exhaustion washed over her, taking with it her appetite for the fight.

Why had she come? What do I really expect to achieve? she asked herself dully.

'This is pointless. I shouldn't have come. I should get back…they'll be wondering…' Her voice trailed away. Had she even told anyone where she was going?

She banged her head with the heel of her hand and screwed up her face in a mask of concentration as she struggled to recall the exact sequence of events that had brought her here.

She was able to recall getting the idea of confronting the man responsible for the nightmare on her way back to the hospital with a change of clothes for Ed; presumably those clothes were still in her car. Her next clear memory was of landing outside this building, but no matter how hard she tried the in between remained fuzzy.

'You were limping?'

Libby glanced down with lack of interest at her throbbing foot. 'It's nothing.'

'Let me be the judge of that.'

'Because I value your opinion so much?' She laughed scornfully at the suggestion and added, 'I turned my ankle, that's all.' It seemed a very long time ago.

'Let me see.'

She looked at the dark head of the man kneeling at her feet and wondered how he got there. She closed her eyes but the room carried on spinning.

'Your foot.'

Libby extended her leg. She was unable to repress a wince of pain as he eased the shoe off her swollen foot.

'That looks painful.'

'It's not too bad.'

Ignoring her protest, he continued to turn her ankle from side to side, viewing the extent of the damage. His touch was clinical but surprisingly gentle. It took him a few minutes before he ventured an opinion.

'I don't think anything is broken.'

'I could have told you that.'

He flashed her a look. 'But I think you'd be a lot more comfortable with a supportive strapping.' He aimed an assessing look at her pale face. 'Wait there.'

Rafael was relieved to find that Gretchen was back at her post. She raised a brow of enquiry. Who knew what garbled story the other woman had told her? But she didn't waste time asking questions when he told her what he needed.

Back in the office he found Libby where he had left her looking if anything even paler. Her expressive eyes turned his way but remained worryingly blank.

He cursed softly under his breath. She had been running on adrenaline and hate and the tank had finally run dry.

'You'll be more comfortable here, I think,' he suggested, nodding towards a sofa—one of a pair set against one wall of his office. He had slept on it himself on more than one occasion when after a late meeting it had not seemed worthwhile going home only to return a couple of hours later.

He was laying her down when Gretchen walked in carrying everything he'd asked for.

'Been making maidens swoon again?'

Rafael acknowledged the riposte with a twisted grin. 'I think it might be a good idea to bring some tea—make it sweet.'

'I'll make it now, and a couple of aspirin?' Gretchen said, glancing at Libby. 'Hello again.'

Libby had to blink hard to bring the woman's face into focus and wondered why the beautiful blonde looked familiar.

'I'm just going to put some ice on this. It will help the swelling.'

Libby winced as the ice touched her bruised skin.

Leaving the compress in place, he selected an appropriate bandage from the first-aid box Gretchen had brought.

Gretchen herself returned a moment later carrying a tray. 'Tea is…too late.' She nodded towards the sleeping girl. 'Out flat. A friend of yours?'

'More an acquaintance,' Rafael said shortly.

'Any idea how she got like this?'

Rafael considered her pale sleeping face, refusing to identify the emotion he felt break free as tenderness. 'Some…'

Gretchen produced a printed slip from her pocket. 'Does this offer any clues?'

It was a boarding pass for a transatlantic flight. Rafael studied the time and date.

'So she was getting off a flight from New York at…' His eyes widened as he bit out a curse. His mental calculations suggested that his vengeful redhead had been on her feet for a hell of a long time.

The surprise was not that she was out for the count, it was that she'd stayed upright as long as she had! Refusing to acknowledge the emotion he felt tighten in his chest, Rafael turned abruptly away.

He had made it a point never to place himself in a position where he felt responsible for someone else; to this end he had successfully avoided emotional ties.

This woman might need a keeper, but it wasn't him.

CHAPTER SIX

LIBBY shook herself free of a deep sleep, stretching like a kitten as she tried to work out where she was and how she got here.

Rafael saw the moment her memory returned.

'Oh, God!' she whispered, sitting bolt upright.

Libby turned in the direction of the drawled, 'Hello there.'

'What have you done to me?'

'Other than drugged you and had my wicked way with you, you mean?' Rafael, who was slouched elegantly in a leather-backed swivel chair, closed the lid of the laptop open on the desk in front of him and got to his feet.

Libby felt the embarrassed colour rush to her cheeks; to say she felt at a disadvantage would have been putting it mildly. She watched under the screen of her lashes as the tall figure shrugged on the jacket slung across the back of his chair and approached exuding an aura of energy. Feeling utterly drained and flat, she felt exhausted just watching him.

If exhaustion was the only thing he made her feel she would have felt a lot happier.

Had he been sitting there watching her? The possibility made her feel vulnerable.

She covered her mouth, unable to repress the drowsy yawn. 'What happened?' It was frustrating not to be able to remember.

'Nothing dramatic. You fell asleep.'

Libby shook her head. 'Why would I fall asleep?'

He raised a brow. 'A tough one that, but let's think, shall we? Could it possibly have anything to do with jet lag, no sleep, no food? Or even all three.' He watched her flush and added as an afterthought, 'And then a large dose of emotional pyrotechnics.'

'Oh!'

He arched an ebony brow. 'Coming back, is it?'

Libby gave a tight-lipped nod and flung a murderous glare his way for good measure.

'I'm very sorry to have inconvenienced you,' she began, swinging her legs to the ground. She broke off, catching sight of the bandage on her ankle.

'Before you ask, I put it there. I think I did a good job but I'd get it checked over with your doctor if I were you.'

'You!'

His stern classical features relaxed into a smile. 'It was my good deed for the day.'

Libby reminded herself that under the smile—it made him look years younger—he was still the same ruthless, cold-blooded predator.

'Am I meant to say thank you?' she enquired, adopting an air of studied disinterest.

'I'd prefer it if you took a deep breath!' He accompanied the command with a cutting motion of his hand. 'And tell me slowly and clearly this time why you are here without the histrionics.'

'I've already told you and I might just as well have talked to that wall.' She nodded towards the white wall lined with a row of artistic monochrome photographs that portrayed wild and rugged seascapes. 'Well, you might not listen but I'm sure there are a lot of people who will.'

Had she felt so inclined she knew it would not be hard—success and scandal were two things that people liked to read about.

She had no intention of taking a route that would expose her own family to the glare of public scrutiny but she saw no reason to share this information with him—let him worry.

Rafael pinned her with a stare that would have made ice cubes look warm.

'A word of advice.'

Libby got stiffly to her feet and planted her hands on her hips. 'You know where you can stick your advice, don't you?' She doubted anyone she knew would have recognised this rude Libby; she barely recognised herself.

'I can guess.' The flicker of amusement again, but this time it seemed forced, only momentarily lightening the grim cast of his extraordinarily handsome face.

But even the suggestion was enough to fuel the flame of her ire, she was being as nasty and abusive as she knew how and he thought it was funny! Short of kick him in the shins—he'd probably kick her back—how did you inflict damage on someone like him?

'I was going to say that if you are going to defame a person's character make sure there are no witnesses. It makes you extremely vulnerable to legal action.'

'Am I meant to be intimidated?' Laughing, Libby tilted her head back to direct her defiant glare at his face. 'I'm only "vulnerable", as you put it, if what I say is not true, so bring it on!' she challenged, wagging a finger at him. 'I'm sure the media would just *love* the story,' she observed as she wiped a hand across her gritty eyes. She had to look a total wreck.

For a split second their eyes connected, glowing gold on swimming blue; suddenly the air between them shimmered with the explosive tension that materialised without warning.

Libby's heart rate quickened; in the moment before he turned abruptly away she saw the shock flicker in his amber eyes and knew he was feeling it too.

Her breath still coming in breathy, uneven gasps, Libby dropped her accusing finger and watched as he walked unhurriedly across to a leather swivel chair set beside his desk. The quiver of appreciation that tightened her stomach muscles as she observed his progress made her deeply ashamed.

She could deal with his threats; the raw, rampant sexuality he exuded was another matter.

Libby barely registered the discomfort as the half moons of her pearly fingernails gouged reddened grooves into the flesh of her palms. She dashed a white-knuckled fist across her eyes. It seemed such a massive betrayal to allow herself to notice that he moved with the innate elegance of a feral creature, let alone be fascinated by it or excited by the leashed power suggested in his smallest action.

Not that it was a matter of *allow*; allow implied there was some sort of choice and Libby did not have choice. That was the scary part—she had no control whatsoever over her reaction. The realisation filled her with a mixture of shame and alarm as she felt her body react to him.

Her firm jaw clenched. She *hated* this happening, and she hated Rafael Alejandro. She struggled to gain some sort of objectivity. This wasn't about the man, it was about the intense physical magnetism he exuded.

Sanity and self-respect lay in separating the two… It *sounded* easy. Who knew she could even feel this way? Who knew that she could look at a man she loathed and think about his hands on her skin, his mouth on her—? Libby shook her head, refusing to complete the thought.

It seemed a good time to remember that she wasn't a very highly sexed person, she never had been—imagine how bad this could be if she were!

She squared her jaw. It was mortifying but it was just something she'd have to endure until this temporary insanity passed or he vanished from her life, whichever came first. She had no doubt at all that both would happen.

She lowered her lashes in a protective screen as he slipped the button of his beautifully cut grey jacket. Underneath he wore a white shirt with a thin silver stripe running through it. His narrow silk tie was the same shade of silver.

The man might be a total reptile, but there was no doubt that he had style and no morals, she reminded herself as she dragged her gaze from the suggestion of muscular ripple as he lifted a hand to rub it back and forth across his dark hair, causing short strands to stand up before he smoothed them back with a preoccupied expression.

What, she wondered, was he preoccupied by— the next person he intended to grind beneath the heel of his handmade leather shoes?

It was massively frustrating, she decided as she struggled and failed miserably to gauge the expression on his lean face. All she could see mirrored in his eyes was her own reflection looking back at her.

Libby sighed. Had she really expected to see a flicker of remorse from the heartless bastard— *beautiful* bastard, she corrected silently as he gracefully folded his long lean length into the chair.

The taut silence that had built up grew thicker as Rafael Alejandro, who appeared oblivious now to the nerve-shredding tension, stretched his long legs out in front of him and leaned further back, pushing his head into the leather headrest as he rested his chin on the platform of his steepled fingers.

Rafael's initial response to her earlier harangue had been outrage—she had offended him on every level—but as she had continued to throw the ludicrous heated accusations at him outrage had receded to be replaced by an equally strong desire to wipe that haughty look of disdain from her face and see it replaced by desire.

Rafael wanted to see those beautiful eyes shimmer, not with loathing, but with helpless lust; he wanted to see those lips, not tight with condemnation, but soft and tremulous in anticipation of his kiss.

Rafael did not doubt his ability to bring about these changes, but why would he? Why should he? She was *exactly* the sort of high-maintenance female he avoided.

There were any number of women who were flatteringly grateful for any attention he gave them, women who were only too eager to tell him how marvellous he was.

Rafael was suddenly filled by a compelling need to hear this spitting red-headed virago tell him how marvellous he was. It was almost as powerful as the desire he felt to feel her soft body beneath him, to hear her soft moan as he parted her lips and plundered all the hot sweetness within.

Libby felt the slow sweep of his eyes as they journeyed with excruciating slowness up from her toes, she felt it like a burning brand. It took all her will power to stand there and endure the insolent leisurely appraisal.

It seemed to Libby it just went on and on. Finally unable to maintain her defiant pose, she snapped.

'Are you marking me out of ten?' The moment the cranky remark left her lips Libby realised she was inviting a massive put-down, and she firmed her slender shoulders in preparation.

The moments stretched and as no put-down was forthcoming she watched warily as his dark lashes lifted, exposing the dark bands of colour along the angles of his high cheekbones. The impact the molten heat burning in his stare had on her drew a gasp from low in her throat and made her stomach muscles clench viciously.

'Fishing...?'

Libby blinked to clear the buzzing in her head. 'A compliment from you?' She made a sound of scorn and curled her lip.

Head tipped a little to one side, he studied her flushed furious face before concluding, 'The sneer could do with some work, but the self-righteous diatribe, now that,' he admitted, shaking his head slowly from side to side in an attitude of mock admiration, 'I was impressed and I am not easily impressed.'

'I can die a happy woman.' And if her heart rate didn't slow, Libby thought, clamping a hand to her chest, that might be sooner than later!

'I particularly like the way you managed to ignore inconvenient things like facts.'

'One *fact*,' she bit out fiercely.

Rafael's laconic drawl cut across her retort.

'Yeah, I know, *querida*, I am the devil's spawn.' He gave a grin that was dangerously close to the role he cast himself. 'And responsible,' he continued, expanding on the mocking theme, 'for everything from global warming to the national debt situation.'

'Responsible,' she corrected grimly, 'for the destruction of my family.'

His brows lifted at the dramatic pronouncement. 'You do not look very *destroyed* to me.' His eyes drifted to her mouth. 'A bit shaky on your feet.' The indent between his dark brows deepened as Rafael noted the almost transparent pallor of her skin, a pallor that emphasised the violet smudges beneath her eyes.

Her vulnerability shone clear through the bolshy pose. Hate and pride were the only things that had got this woman back on her feet, Rafael realised as he fought off a strong and totally uncharacteristic urge to pull her into his arms.

Rafael had learned, admittedly not quickly enough to save himself from a couple of beatings and being left literally penniless, to subdue his compassionate instincts. Falling for a sob story and a sad face, even a pretty one, was not a good survival instinct for a teenager fending for himself.

Instead of opening his arms Rafael pulled out a chair. It was far safer and he was no longer a boy with chivalrous ideals intact.

Libby, even though her knees were shaking, ignored the unspoken invitation with a sniff.

'Would you like a drink? Tea? Coffee?'

Libby swallowed the knot of emotion lodged like a boulder in her aching throat, her jaw tightening as she silently vowed not to give him the satisfaction of seeing her cry.

'I did not come here for a cup of tea.'

'So why did you come?'

Libby blinked and thought, Good question. 'We've already covered that and the really tragic thing is you still don't have a clue.' She shook her head slowly from side to side in an attitude of weary disbelief.

'Have you ever cared about anyone but yourself? You haven't even got the guts to admit when you're in the wrong,' she charged in disgust. 'You're completely…' She stopped and thought, What's the point?

His brows lifted. 'Completely what?'

'Forget it.'

'It's a bit late to worry about my feelings. Say what you think, don't hold back, *querida*,' he drawled.

His mockery sent a fresh rush of re-energising adrenaline through Libby's body. 'I'm not worried about your feelings!' It was news to her that he had any. 'Fine!' He wanted to know, she'd tell him. 'I think you'd do anything including sell your own grandmother to make a profit, you don't care who you hurt getting what you want, wouldn't know a scruple if it bit you and…and…and…' suddenly intensely weary, she felt her anger drain away, leaving her feeling flat and utterly exhausted '…and don't call me that!' she finished lamely.

He raised a sardonic brow and got to his feet in one lazy fluid motion. Libby took an involuntary step backwards, sucking in a shocked little breath.

Rafael's glance slid to the blue-veined pulse

throbbing at the base of her throat. In his mind he was running his tongue across the skin there, tasting the salt, tasting her... He blinked to clear the distracting image, unable to recall when he had been so totally consumed by hunger for a woman.

He refused to over-analyse. It was no mystery, just sex. And sex had never been a problem for him. It was relationships that Rafael ran shy of, at first because they required time and energy he had needed to focus to succeed, and later when he had established himself he realised that a life with no emotional encumbrances, no emotional dramas, suited him.

He had lived pretty much all his life out of a suitcase, rarely staying in one place more than a few months, never long enough to put down roots or form close friendships, and domesticity held very little charm for him.

He was always upfront with women, never pretended he wanted more than a physical relationship. Rafael had become an expert at reading the signs, knowing when a woman felt she was *the one*.

Her reaction appeared to amuse him. 'I don't bite, *querida*.' His sensuous lips tugged upwards into a lazy smile that sent Libby's stomach into a lurching dive. 'Unless of course requested.'

Libby shivered even though the purring addition had sent her core temperature up several degrees. She wanted to respond to the voice in her head that was shrieking, 'Run,' but pride wouldn't allow her to.

Libby, eyes narrowed, took a step forward to regain the ground lost by her retreat both literally and figuratively, determined to show that she wasn't intimidated by him in any way.

A gleam flashed amusement and his grin deepened as he murmured approvingly, 'Good girl.' She might be a spoilt little rich girl, but if Marchant had as much guts and loyalty as his daughter the situation might have turned out very differently.

'Your *approval*—my life is complete,' she said sarcastically.

CHAPTER SEVEN

'THAT'S going a bit far, but I do think you have… potential. And I really don't think you want to get into the game of assigning guilt because if you did the subject of your father's loose grasp of the most basic rules of business arise.'

Rafael's scorn stung Libby. 'My father is twice the man you will ever be!'

He appeared unperturbed by the charge. 'Possibly,' he conceded.

'And it's not Dad's fault, a lot of businesses are suffering, it's the economic downturn, he just needed time—'

'To do what? Play another round of golf?'

Libby reacted angrily to the scorn in his voice. 'My father blames himself for what has happened. He feels responsible for the people who are losing their jobs.'

'He is right to blame himself,' Rafael, who had studied the numbers, retorted.

Libby responded with protective anger. 'If my father is such a loser why did your grandfather have faith in him?'

'I am sure he had his reasons.'

The contempt etched into his face made her see red. 'None that you'd understand,' she flung back. 'Your grandfather was a decent man. It's a pity you didn't inherit some of his integrity.'

During the short static silence that followed her outburst Libby watched the muscle in his lean cheek clenching. She could actually not take her eyes off it—or him.

His expression was like stone as he turned and began to walk over to the big antique desk that dominated the room.

Libby watched him warily, mystified as much about the suppressed emotions he was emanating as his actions. Her bewilderment deepened as he took a key from his pocket and, without a word, fitted it to a drawer in the desk.

His dark lashes lay across the sharp angle of his

jutting cheekbones, effectively screening his expression from her curious gaze. Frustrated, Libby watched as he appeared to scan the top sheet of the sheaf of papers he extracted from the drawer. She started slightly as he turned on his heel and began to walk back across the room towards her with them in his hand.

There was a pronounced sneer of distaste stamped on his lean patrician features as Rafael dropped the papers in her lap. 'This is my grandfather's integrity,' he drawled. 'Go on, take a look,' he urged. 'I think you will find it educational.'

Libby stared at the papers. 'I don't understand.' Her face lifted to his. 'What are they?'

'It is a contract between my grandfather and a development company.'

She gave a bewildered shrug. 'What has that got to do with me?'

Rafael leaned across and, turning to the second typed page, he stabbed his forefinger on the relevant word. 'Does that look familiar?' he asked, lifting his hand away.

Pushing the damp curls from her face with one

hand, she looked down at the passage he had pointed to. 'Is all this mystery stuff really necessary?' She picked up the papers and waved them at him. 'Why can't you just say what is so...?'

A word on a fluttering page caught her attention and Libby stopped mid-sentence, snatching the page in question free of the binder.

'How...how is this possible? The house... What—' she demanded in a quavering voice '—is this?' She lifted her gaze, her eyes brushing his before dropping back to the paper.

'It is an agreement drawn up between my grandfather and a development company signed, sealed and just awaiting the signatures. Unfortunately for Aldo he died before he had a chance to call in the loan he gave your father, which had always been his intention.'

Pale as paper, Libby shook her head in a negative motion of rejection. 'No!'

The muscles along Rafael's strong jaw tightened as he drew in a shuddering breath through flared nostrils. Her refusal to abandon her belief in his grandfather's integrity and her readiness to assign the worst possible motives to him evoked a seething frustration.

Libby's fingers trembled as she turned a page, and she gasped when she saw the figure that leapt out at her. 'But it's not worth that much—nowhere near,' she protested as she breathed through a wave of nausea.

Rafael met her startled gaze and provided a simple explanation for the staggering amount on the page.

'With planning permission for an out-of-town shopping complex a formality, it is worth that much…almost certainly more. My grandfather had an over-inflated opinion of his ability but any half-decent businessman would have got a better price.'

Libby, white-faced and shaking with the impact of these revelations, struggled to take on board this information. The home she had loved was to be turned into a shopping centre?

'They want to knock down our house?' If this was true, did Rafael plan to follow through with this diabolical scheme? 'But this *can't* be right.

Your grandfather was helping Dad—he was his friend.'

'My grandfather never put friendship ahead of profit in his life. When he offered your father a loan he knew that he would be unable to repay it and your father didn't examine Aldo's motives too deeply because he wanted an easy way out, and not one that required any sacrifice or work on his part. He is a lazy man who inherited a healthy business and ran it into the ground. He enjoyed seeing his name on the letterhead that appears to have been the limit of his enthusiasm.'

'My father put his family ahead of his work.' Unlike some of her friends' fathers, her dad had always been there; he never worked late.

'Your father put *everything* ahead of his work.'

Libby, shaking her head, lowered her gaze.

There was some sympathy in his eyes as he studied her downbent head. 'You know what I'm saying is true.'

Libby compressed her lips and felt guilty as hell because he was right; she had recognised that there was a grain of truth in his accusations. 'At least my dad wasn't a crook!' Her eyes narrowed. 'And he's not a callous bastard like you.'

'Oh, my grandfather never did anything illegal.' Aware that the charge of callousness had been aimed at him, Rafael did not attempt to deny the charge.

Her eyes shot wide. 'And you think that makes it all right? How proud your grandfather must have been of you. A regular chip off the old block,' she jeered.

Unprepared for his reaction to her words, Libby physically recoiled from the lick of white-hot rage she glimpsed in his compelling deep-set eyes. But more disturbing than this was the low, almost feral sound that was dragged from Rafael's throat. It made the hair on the back of her neck stand on end.

'I was nothing to him, and he was less than nothing to me.' Nostrils flared, he snapped his fingers expressively.

Conscious that she had inadvertently hit a nerve, Libby knew the sensible thing would be to back off; instead she heard herself say belligerently,

'It looks to me like you had no problem steeping into his shoes.'

'I inherited nothing from my grandfather.'

Libby, who could not let this pass unchallenged, gave a snort and waved an accusing arm around the big room. 'Nothing except all this.' Her scornful gaze settled back on his lean face. 'You're such a hypocrite!' she charged contemptuously. 'A pathetic hypocrite!'

A look of utter astonishment crossed his features that on another occasion might have made her laugh.

'Madre di Dios...!'

'What's wrong?' she taunted. 'You can dish it out but you can't take it?'

His eyes narrowed on her face. 'Try me.' He accompanied the invitation with a 'bring it on' gesture.

Libby, her eyes narrowed, obliged. 'Where do you get off criticising my dad, looking down your nose at him for inheriting his money, when compared to the silver spoon you were born with—'

'I was not born with a silver spoon.'

The harsh rebuttal drew a laugh from Libby. 'No, solid gold.'

'It happens to be true. My grandfather did not choose to acknowledge my existence until two years ago.'

Libby's blue eyes flew wide. 'Why—what did you do?'

'I was born.' He arched a sardonic brow and studied the face turned up to him. 'Not so colourful a sin as you were anticipating, I suspect.'

Libby gave an uncomfortable shrug and felt foolish as she heard him add heavily, 'But one that in my grandfather's eyes was unforgivable.'

She struggled to banish the lingering image of a lonely, rejected little boy from her head—empathy was the last thing she wanted to feel for this man... Well, maybe not the last, but it was right up there with blind, indiscriminate lust.

'So you were—'

When she broke off, colouring uncomfortably, Rafael, looking amused, finished the sentence for her. 'A bastard, yes, I am. I was the result of an affair my mother had with a married man when she was seventeen.' Rafael had never felt the desire to seek out the man who had rejected him. He had not even known the man's name until he went through his mother's pitiably meagre personal effects after her death and found his birth certificate.

'And my grandfather threw her out, he washed his hands of her. When he contacted me two years ago he didn't even know she was dead—that is how interested he was.'

The casually delivered information horrified Libby. 'She was only seventeen, his own daughter, how could he do that?' Her bewilderment was genuine.

Rafael shook his head and looked amused. 'You have a very romanticised view of families.'

'I think I've just been lucky,' she admitted.

The softness in her voice was mirrored in the blue eyes looking at him. With a sense of profound shock Rafael identified the emotion swimming in the cerulean depths.

'Relying on luck appears to be a family failing.'

Having successfully doused the glow of sympathy in her eyes with the sly insert, he gave an almost imperceptible nod of satisfaction. Pity from anyone, least of all a beautiful woman, was not something that Rafael could stomach, even as he acknowledged, allowing his gaze to move over the soft contours of her face, she was beautiful.

Libby's chin lifted in reaction to his mockery. 'I think roots are important and family loyalty, but I wouldn't expect you to understand that,' she charged, injecting her voice with scorn.

The hard lines of his bronzed features tightened as he suggested contemptuously, 'Being a bastard makes me incapable of appreciating such things…?'

Libby's gaze did not drop. 'Don't put words in my mouth. And for the record if I ever call you a bastard I won't be referring to the circumstances of your birth!'

Her angry retort drew his restless glowing gaze to her lips. This time Libby did look away from the predatory gleam in his incredible eyes, her heart pounding so hard she didn't see how he couldn't hear it. She watched the knuckles of her clenched fingers blench white as she struggled to regain a semblance of composure.

It was mortifying to be forced to acknowledge she was sexually attracted to a man she hated and despised, but then maybe all women felt forbidden cravings when they looked at Rafael...?

She was sure a lot looked.

'I have been called worse, but not recently.'

Libby's gaze lifted and she was perplexed by the amusement etched in his dark features. Why did this man never react the way she expected?

'And for the record I have inherited little that was not already mine. When my grandfather died I was already the majority holder in his company and poised to launch a takeover.' His broad shoulders lifted as his sensual lips curved into a cynical smile. 'His dying simply saved me the trouble.'

Libby's wide gaze connected with his cold, implacable eyes and she gave a horrified shudder. 'You deliberately set out to ruin your own grandfather.'

'He would hardly have been penniless and destitute.'

'Just humiliated?'

Not appearing even slightly discomposed by the suggestion, Rafael ran a hand down the hard curve of his smooth shaven jaw.

'Let us say that on this occasion financial gain was not my sole motivation.'

A man who showed such ruthlessness when it came to his own family was not, she realised with a sinking heart, going to show her own family any pity.

'Did he ever apologise?'

'That would have been hard considering that he never laid eyes on me.' And you are telling her all this, Rafael, why exactly?

'You *never* met him?'

'No.'

'But you said he tried to contact you two years ago—'

Rafael swept a hand across his brow and clicked his tongue irritably. 'He did, but not out of any desire to make up for the years of neglect. He suggested a financial merger.' The offer had been laughable, hardly worth dignifying with a response.

But he had responded—through an intermediary.

'I don't know how anyone could do that.'

'Sleep with a married man, princess?'

'No,' she snapped, annoyed at his interpretation. 'Disown your own child. Did she and your father ever—?' She stopped, embarrassed.

'You wish to know if there was a happy ending, whether my parents were eventually happily united.' He shook his head. 'Outside the pages of fiction happy endings are rare,' he observed cynically. 'There was no happy ending. The man did not want to know—'

'Your father, you mean.'

'It takes more than impregnation to make a father,' he retorted quietly. 'My mother left Europe for South America with a lover.'

'Your stepfather?'

'While I realise that my family is a fascinating subject, it is not what we are here to discuss.' The reminder was as much for his own benefit as hers.

'Rafael.' Libby paused—she had called him by his name for the first time. It felt…*strange*, she decided, resisting the silly impulse to say it again. 'Give my father time to—'

'I do not put sentiment ahead of good business practice or throw good money after bad.'

The hard inflection in his voice made Libby grit her teeth as she fought despair. She squared her shoulders and tried another tack. 'I'm not asking for charity, I'm asking—no, actually I'm *demanding* that you give us time.'

Unwilling admiration flickered in his eyes. 'Some people would have begged, but you demand. Does that usually work for you?' Without giving her an opportunity to respond, he added, 'Time to what?'

'Turn things around.'

He arched a brow. 'We?'

'My brother, me…I've got—'

'No interest in business. Shall we talk bottom line? Your father inherited a successful business and he has run it into the ground simply because he is either unwilling or unable to adapt. When he got into trouble he did not seek advice, he did not alter his pleasant lifestyle or that of his family. There were no economies, instead he borrowed and then borrowed some more.'

When he put it like that it did sound pretty bad. 'We can't all be a financial genius.'

'We can't all be born with a silver spoon in our pretty mouths,' he returned, his eyes on her lips. 'This is the real world, *querida*, bad things happen to nice people and not so nice people also. Not to mention stupid people—yes, I do mean your father.'

'What else would you call a man who relies on miracles instead of strategies? He made no effort whatever to control his overspending. Why do you want this business to survive? Your brother has no interest in it and you...'

'Me?'

'You are not involved, You apparently had no idea that your father was in financial difficulties?'

Libby's chin went up a defensive inch at the underlying criticism she sensed in his question. 'Of course not.'

'But if you had you would have offered to help.'

'Of course!'

'And if I give you that chance now…?'

Confused, she frowned warily. 'A chance to what?'

'A chance to work here, see how a business should be run, learn from experts…'

'Me work for you!' she exclaimed, waiting for the punchline.

When it did not come she shook her head. 'I'm assuming that is your idea of a joke.'

He shrugged. 'You wanted a chance and I am giving you one.'

'So you said, but giving me a chance to *what*?'

'Prove there is more to you than a pretty face.'

Her lips tightened at the implication she was some decorative dummy. 'I have nothing to prove. I graduated…I have a job.'

He angled a sardonic ebony brow. 'A job that pays well enough for you to fly to New York and back business class? Impressive,' he drawled.

Libby's lips compressed as her glance slid from his. 'The flight was a gift from my parents.'

'And this job—was that too a present from Mummy and Daddy, by any chance?'

Her indignant gaze jerked upwards. 'No!'

'So you went through the interview process...'

A mortified wave of colour washed over her fair skin but she refused to drop her gaze this time. 'The editor of the paper I work for—'

'I had no idea I was talking to a journalist.'

She bit her lip—he was taunting her. 'It's a local free sheet,' she said, honesty compelling her to add, 'I cover small stuff, fêtes, school plays, football matches. My grandfather started the paper—he wanted to give something back to the community.'

'So given your history your fellow applicants could be excused for thinking you had an advantage—'

'All right, there were no other applicants and I didn't interview. Mike has known me since I was a kid. I've got a degree in English Lit—he knew I could do the job with my eyes closed.'

'Of course he did,' Rafael drawled. 'And let me guess, he plays golf with your father?'

Libby's jaw dropped. 'How did you know that?'

Rafael laughed outright at her astonishment. 'Call it a wild guess. Have you ever stretched yourself, actually attempted anything outside your comfort zone?'

Stung by the look of contemptuous amusement he sent her way, Libby flared back, 'Plenty of times!'

'Like the job you can do with your eyes closed...?'

Libby gritted her teeth as she suffered the humiliation of having her own words used to condemn her. 'I wasn't being literal.'

'Don't you ever get bored?'

The colour in her cheeks deepened at the scorn in his voice. 'So I live at home,' she yelled. 'And, yes, I *don't* have some high-powered job. But there's more to life than making money and the last time I checked it's not a criminal offence not to be particularly ambitious.'

'You've never had to work for anything in your life, have you? It's all been handed you on a plate by parents who—'

Eyes flashing fire, she cut across him. 'You can poke fun at me if you like but leave my parents out of this. Of course they're protective— who wouldn't be if they'd had a kid who spent more time in hospital than at home?' She stopped abruptly and thought, Too much information, Libby.

'You were ill as a child?'

Libby summed up the frequent journeys in ambulances, several admissions to the paediatric intensive care unit and innumerable stays on the ward where everyone knew her name in a brief sentence.

'I had asthma—it was difficult to control.' She threw him a guarded look. 'I grew out of it.'

To her surprise he let the subject drop beyond a brief comment of, 'I believe this sometimes happens.

'You show any potential, convince me in the next month that you are capable and I will finance this recovery.'

Libby was astonished by the offer. 'But why?'

He shrugged. 'I am feeling generous.'

She viewed him through suspicious narrowed eyes. 'Because you're *such* a philanthropist.'

'So you think I have an angle?'

She would not, he conceded, be far wrong. His motives were at best mixed.

It was true that she had managed to tweak his conscience, but not to the extent that he considered his decision had been wrong. It was entirely possible, had he not spent the time she had been sleeping wondering how he was going to get her into bed, he might have ignored that tweak totally.

That he was going to get her into his bed was not a question he had wasted any energy over, it was a given and had been from the moment he had looked at her and experienced the most primal reaction he had ever had for a woman.

'I think you wouldn't recognise a straight line if it was drawn across your forehead.' Too much truth, Libby! Fully anticipating her jibe would elicit an offended counter-attack, she was startled when he loosed a low growl of laughter.

She stared at him, trying hard not to notice how warm and inviting his eyes looked when they were filled with genuine humour.

CHAPTER EIGHT

'HAVE I got this right—you're offering me a job?'

Libby struggled to get her head around it. When she had stormed her way into his office her aims had not gone beyond the desire to experience the extreme satisfaction of telling Rafael Alejandro *exactly* what she thought of him with the outside possibility she might awake whatever he had that passed for a conscience.

She hadn't expected a U-turn or for him to lie awake nights filled with remorse, and equally she definitely hadn't expected this!

A second chance!

Or was it?

'An internship.'

Libby digested this information and resisted the strong temptation to scream *yes, please* before he changed his mind. There was such a thing as being too eager and, even more importantly, there was such a thing as walking into danger with your eyes closed.

This man, she mused, had danger written all over him. 'You expect me to work for you for free?'

Rafael gave a smile. Her voice gave away none of her feelings, but her white knuckles did, at least to someone as adept at reading body language as he was.

'Free?' He directed a quizzical look at her composed face. 'Delaying the closure is not worth anything to you?' He shook his head and evinced amazement. 'I have to tell you, *querida*, that internships with me are highly sought after.' The high-flying graduates who often arrived with a high opinion of themselves had any illusions they had landed a cushy number knocked out of them quickly, and those that didn't…well, there were always far more eager applicants than there were places.

Rafael firmly believed that everyone should

have equal opportunities for advancement in the workplace.

'I'm sure they are,' she admitted, losing her cool and flushing with embarrassment. 'It's just—'

'You have no ambition, no—' his heavy-lidded eyes slid to her lips '—hunger…'

'I have hunger!' she protested fiercely.

'I am pleased to hear it.' And he could not wait to feel it, feel her eager hands on his body and her starving lips on his skin.

He gave an exaggerated shrug and walked with fluid grace across the room towards the window to hide the blatant evidence of his arousal.

A distracted expression slid across Libby's face as she watched the light catch his hair, burnishing it to a blue-black sheen. Did it feel as silky as it looked?

'You want to do it?'

Want? She wanted to run in the opposite direction. 'When you say internship…? You mean?'

'I mean internship, a learning process, initially shadowing—'

A mental image of following him around all day

flashed into Libby's head. 'You?' she interrupted, thinking a few minutes in his company and she was a basket case, twenty-four seven didn't bear thinking about.

'You know what they say, keep your friends close.' A slow predatory smile spread across his lean face, and his eyes remained brooding as his voice dropped to a throaty purr as he added, 'And your enemies closer, *querida*,' reminding Libby of a large sleek cat tormenting a mouse.

She struggled to shake the feeling she was being manipulated. You're in control, Libby, this is your call—you're in control.

She believed it right up to the point where she looked at his mouth.

Her stomach muscles gave a traitorous quiver—just how close was he talking about? Was this talk of internships some euphemism?

'How close?' she asked bluntly.

'*Close?*'

Libby scowled at this blatantly bogus show of bewilderment. 'Are you expecting me to sleep with you to get my dad a second chance?'

'Some people might consider the question crude, but I find your directness most attractive. However, when discussing sex I find it is always polite to wait until you're asked, *querida*.' His smile deepened as he watched the hot mortified colour rush to her already pink cheeks.

'I just...I thought—'

Taking pity on her discomfiture, he cut across her mortified mumble. 'As we are being frank, in answer to your question, yes, I do *expect* you to sleep with me. You look shocked.'

Libby stared. 'How do you expect me to look? Do I look to you like someone who would trade sexual favours to get what I want? There's a name for people who do that.'

A flicker of impatience crossed his lean features. 'Do not be dramatic—there is no question of trading anything. It has been obvious from the first moment we met that we would end up in bed.' There was nothing in his manner to suggest he had said anything out of the ordinary as his bold stare settled on Libby's face.

For a moment the sheer, unadulterated arrogance

of the man struck her dumb. When her voice did return it had developed a husky, breathless quality that made her frown.

'You need therapy!'

No, he needed sex. Three months was too long to go without for a man with a healthy libido, and pressure of work was not a valid excuse. A man did not stop taking in calories because he was busy, not even if the food on offer had a boring sameness.

His sex life had become if not boring certainly unsurprising; he knew that Libby Marchant was not going to bore him. She was not the only one who needed some challenge in her life.

'I get that you're the sort of man who feels obliged to prove he's a man by hitting on anything in a skirt and hate to spoil your little fantasy—' she began in an icy tone of withering contempt.

A contemplative smile tugged the corners of his sensually sculpted lips upwards. 'No, not little,' he protested. 'It has actually become quite detailed.'

Refusing to acknowledge his throaty interruption, she clenched her teeth and continued to deliver her scornful analysis of his character.

'But the only thing that is *obvious* to me is that you think a hell of a lot of yourself.'

Probably with some justification!

Shamed by the liquid rush of excitement low in her belly, Libby took a quivering breath and drew herself to her full height, wishing as she did so that she had more than an adequate but not impressive five five to face up to his towering six feet five of virile Latin machismo.

'I do not indulge in casual sex.'

'Me neither, *querida*. I am *always* serious about sex.' His eyes drifted to her mouth and the mockery faded from them. 'But I see from your expression that you mean you do not indulge in shallow emotionless sex—let me guess. You only sleep with men who you feel respect for.'

The boredom in his drawl brought a sting of angry colour to her cheeks.

'I will be frank. I *only* indulge in emotionless sex.'

'What am I meant to do—applaud?'

He grinned at her interruption. 'I feel confident we will find some middle ground.'

'Because you're so good at compromises. Look, spare me the details of your love life,' she begged, angling a look of loathing at his lean face, adding, 'And I use the word loosely.' Ignoring Rafael's laugh, she added, 'Because I have a very strong gag reflex!'

This time his throaty laughter was impossible to ignore, in part due to the fact it made her stomach muscles quiver.

'You laugh, but the fact is I'm not going to sleep with you. I have never *not* been going to do anything more!'

His shoulders lifted in a fluid shrug. 'We will see, but relax, the offer is not conditional on that. Call me old-fashioned—I prefer in general not to mix business with pleasure and, no matter how good you are in bed, it will not make me not finance a recovery if you do not make the grade. And just for the record you will know when I'm asking.'

Libby's hands clenched at her sides. 'I wouldn't

sleep with you if you were the last man on the planet!' she blurted in a driven voice.

'Such vehemence!' he admired. 'But who are you trying to convince? Is it possible that your reluctance stems from a fear you will not be able to resist me?'

Libby sucked in a furious breath and stuck out her chin. Aware even as she announced firmly, 'I'll take the job,' that she had been shamelessly manipulated. 'When do I start?'

'Monday morning, nine a.m. sharp.'

CHAPTER NINE

LIBBY hung the boxed pleat skirt she had not previously worn because her mum, when asked for
her opinion, had called it 'middle-aged'—she was
right—on the hanger and placed it next to the
boxy Chanel-style jacket with big silver buttons
she had finally teamed it with.

The outfit was not horrendous, it just had a sexy
quotient of minus ten—the result was exactly
what Libby had been aiming for.

These clothes were not the sort of items someone who intended to sleep with their boss wore,
especially when the boss in question looked
like Rafael Alejandro, a man who had gorgeous
women in short skirts waiting for him to click his
fingers before jumping to the desired height, or
into his bed.

He could have any woman he wanted—she

recalled the raw hunger in his eyes—*and he wants me.*

Every time the thought popped into her head—too often—Libby experienced a shameful spill of liquid heat low in her stomach. The jumbled mixture of confusing emotions that came with this shameful heat deepened her growing sense of dread.

Or was that excitement?

Working on the principle that actions, or in this case clothes, spoke louder than words, Libby was hoping that her selection of outfit would save her the trouble of delivering the speech she had been practicing—the one that included a section on the law that was there to specifically protect employees from the lecherous attentions of the men who employed them.

Having a positive plan in place made her feel more secure until the voice in her head made another unwelcome contribution.

And what's going to protect you from your own hormones, Libby?

And then the whole cycle of panic and doubt with a mingling of guilt began again.

The entire weekend had in fact been a total nightmare! Her mum was struggling to put a brave face on things but even a brave smile and make-up could not hide tear stains.

Her dad had spent most of the time locked in his study. He hadn't washed or dressed and when he did emerge from behind the locked door he hardly said a word.

Ed might have been able to get through to him, if he'd been there Libby might have been tempted to offload her own problems on her level-headed brother, but Ed had spent most of the weekend at the hospital so she had been left to work things out for herself.

Some people reached for a bottle when they had a problem; Libby headed for the kitchen. She found being elbow deep in flour and the smell of baking therapeutic and soothing, but not this time. She had produced enough cookies and brownies to feed an army and still felt no more certain about what she was doing.

Was the offer genuine...?

Did she want it to be?

Could she do it, bearing in mind that she would have to see the man, be polite to him, pretend that he hadn't propositioned her in the most brazen way imaginable?

Pretend that she hadn't considered it, not in a serious way, but *wondered*—she was only human—what would it be like to be touched by a man like that...?

Not that she had any intention of finding out, no—if this offer turned out to be legitimate she was going to make her position clear from the outset; if he laid a finger on her she would sue the pants off him!

An unfortunate analogy considering her tendency to mentally undress him.

She made her plans all the time conscious that her precautions might be unnecessary, that there was a very real possibility that she might turn up and find nobody at the Alejandro building knew who she was, but while there was even the slightest possibility she could save the family from financial ruin she had no choice but to at least find out, even at the risk of a moment or two of toe-curling embarrassment.

Unwilling to raise her family's hopes until things were clearer, she had told them the paper was sending her to cover a trade conference in the City.

For someone who wanted to write fiction, she realised that her powers of invention needed a bit of work, though her brother and parents had too much on their minds to question someone who normally covered fêtes and supermarket openings being asked to report on a conference or, for that matter, a local paper wanting to devote space between the wedding announcements and details of farmers' markets to international trade.

When she had arrived at the Alejandro building that morning Libby's hands had been shaking with a combination of trepidation and excitement.

Now as she smoothed down the pencil skirt she had changed into they were shaking with anger.

She glanced in the full-length mirror and checked the pins that held her hair at her nape in a simple chignon. The voltage of her upbeat smile dimmed as she allowed the façade to slip and gave a snort of self-disgust. Why had she thought for even one minute that his offer was on the level?

'I can do this,' she growled between clenched teeth. 'And it could have been worse,' she reminded herself, mentally replacing the dark tailored trousers, matching waistcoat and plain white silk shirt she was now wearing with a saucy maid's apron and short skirt.

The image pulled the corners of her mouth upwards as she vented a laugh that just stayed the safe side of hysteria as she struggled to see the funny side of the situation. A sense of humour, she reflected grimly, might be the only thing that was going to get her through today with her sanity intact.

A sense of humour was something that Melanie, from Human Resources, had *not* displayed when Libby had exclaimed, *'You've got to be joking!'*

Clearly a literally minded woman, she had looked mildly exasperated and consulted her clipboard before returning her frowning attention back to Libby. 'I understood this was your size.'

Libby glanced at the label sewn into the shirt, then at the trousers. She was a size ten top and size eight bottom; so was the uniform she was holding.

'It is my size. The size isn't the problem.' The problem was the thought of a pair of amber eyes sizing up her vital statistics so accurately.

In response to the older woman's questioning look—at this stage she had still hoped that this was some mild screw-up—and not wanting to get anyone in trouble, she had explained, 'I'm not actually part of a catering team. This is my first day as an intern…'

The woman had directed a puzzled look at Libby. *'And…?'*

Then it had dawned on Libby. 'You expect me to serve drinks?'

'Oh, nothing alcoholic,' Melanie from HR had replied as though the *type* of beverage were Libby's problem. 'This is a working brunch and very informal, just a thank you from Mr

Alejandro to the team that have been working out the details for the first Alejandro trade summit.'

Somehow Libby had stood there, heard the woman blather on proudly about how this event was set to become a yearly international event—as if she cared—and not screamed or broken the furniture.

She was discovering new depths of self-control!

Libby could have stormed out of the building right there and then; she had wanted to, it was only the knowledge that this was exactly what the sadistic, twisted rat wanted her to do that had prevented her.

Genuine! Rafael Alejandro was about as genuine as the smile she had glued on her face.

Aware that the other woman was waiting for a response instead she had forced herself to say, 'I didn't realise.' That makes me a total gullible idiot.

But she'd have the last laugh, Libby thought, managing not a laugh but a very creditable hoarse croak as she lifted her chin to a defiant angle and approached the door of the changing room.

Rafael had obviously expected her to throw some sort of spoiled-princess-afraid-to-get-her-hands-dirty hissy fit…and confirm his view that she was some spoilt airhead. The wretched man was used to pulling strings and having people dance—well, not this time, boss, she thought grimly.

This was no longer about saving the firm—that had obviously always been some sort of twisted joke—this was about pride and she would be the best damned waiter he had ever seen.

If she walked it would be at his invitation and not before.

When Libby got to the big top-floor room people had already begun to arrive, singly and in groups. Some were already helping themselves to the food in the silver-topped servers.

Rafael was not there as yet, her racing heart slowed in reaction to the reprieve.

The person in charge, a silver-haired man wearing a black suit, appeared at her elbow; he did not comment on her lateness as he explained that her brief was to make sure the coffee supply did not run out.

'Offer top-ups, but do not be intrusive.'

And she had been afraid that she would not be up to the job!

As she went about her task Libby kept an eye on the door. She was so jumpy that she messed up the simple task she had been given and slopped half a pot of coffee over the pristine white cloth that covered the tables arranged buffet style along one wall.

Blushing and apologising profusely, she grabbed a napkin from a stack and began to dab at the spreading stain, stepping back with a grimace as the liquid dripped onto her shoes.

The brief hush that fell was not, as she first thought, because everyone was staring at her making a simple task look like brain surgery, but because Rafael had appeared in time to witness her humiliation.

As her eyes brushed those of the tall dynamic figure framed in the doorway her shaking hand sent a half-filled cup flying.

Libby gave a cry. The sound was closely followed by an even louder smashing noise of breaking crockery and the jeering laughter of some smug junior exec whom she had given the brush-off to earlier.

If all eyes had not been on her they were now. Libby stood frozen to the spot with horror while she felt the tide of hot mortification spread across every inch of her skin.

Any hotter and she'd add to the mess on the floor.

'If you could just step back.'

She responded to the calm invitation and watched as the soiled linen was removed and replaced. Within seconds all trace of the mess had been removed and the low buzz of conversation had started up.

'Relax, accidents happen.'

Not to me, not today! Libby bit back the wail and smiled in genuine gratitude at the grey-haired figure who had orchestrated the mop-up operation.

'I'm so sorry.'

He smiled at her, nodded at someone over her shoulder and moved away.

Libby closed her eyes. She knew before she turned who she would see standing there, and her instincts had not failed her.

A serene smile painted on her face to cover the humiliation burning through her veins, she turned to face the tall, imposing figure of Rafael Alejandro. He must have enjoyed seeing her make a total fool of herself.

'Coffee, sir?' she said, aiming the question at a point over his shoulder.

Rafael arched a dark brow and turned to the younger man beside him whose presence Libby had not until this point even registered. Her attention had all been focused on the man she had intended to impress with her efficiency.

Well that went well, Libby.

'What did you think, Callum—should we risk it?' Despite the gentle jibe Rafael had not taken any pleasure from witnessing her public embarrassment. On the contrary he had been impressed by the way she had lifted her chin when the smirking idiot had laughed, after she had flinched. It was at that point that Rafael had had to restrain an uncharacteristic impulse to rush protectively to her side.

Through a miasma of misery Libby heard the other man laugh, but not unkindly. 'I'd love a top-up,' he said, adding, 'We've all been there.'

Libby flashed him a smile of gratitude and thought, Except Rafael, as she tried and failed to imagine the elegant Spaniard messing anything up except other people's lives.

The other man grinned, unwittingly echoing Libby's thoughts as he added drily, 'Not Rafael, of course.'

Irritation moved at the back of Rafael's eyes. 'Rumours of my infallibility have been grossly exaggerated. I'll take a coffee.'

As she filled the cup he held out Libby's hand shook. Rafael's eyes travelled from her small trembling hand to her stiff frozen features and he felt like a total bastard.

The opinion was shared by the voice of his troubled conscience.

Why *troubled*? She was here voluntarily and he was treating her the same way he treated all the interns. It was a method he had used after an intern with a particularly high opinion of himself had caused a lot of bad feeling with his know-it-all attitude; now everyone's first day was spent on the very bottom rung.

Libby was relieved when she was forced to step to one side to allow a tall woman wearing a red suit that made her stand out amongst the more sober hues approach Rafael.

That the most attractive woman in the room made a beeline for Rafael was not exactly a surprise—the surprise would have been if she hadn't!

Libby, despite a near miss when she heard the woman in the red dress laugh throatily in response to something Rafael had said, managed to get through the rest of the service without further incident, possibly because Rafael only stayed for about five minutes after which miraculously her co-ordination returned enough to receive a word of praise from the man in charge when he came to tell her she should leave early to attend the requisite session on health and safety.

Halfway to her destination she realised that she was happy because someone had told her she was quite good at serving coffee.

She began to laugh out loud.

'It is always good to see someone happy in their work.'

Libby, no longer laughing, stopped dead.

'I had the feeling back there that you wanted to say something to me.'

Libby shrugged. 'Just that you're a total bastard.' She closed her eyes and thought, You couldn't keep your mouth shut, could you, Libby?

'In that case I admire your restraint.'

She opened her eyes and thought, To hell with restraint. I've already blown it. 'So do I, I admire me, and my restraint a lot—my restraint,' she bellowed, 'it's just…just legendary. I was incredibly polite to a bunch of patronising idiots in suits who didn't even notice me and I'm not even being paid for it, and for the record serving coffee is not as easy as it looks. Whatever you pay those people it is not enough!' She paused to catch her breath. Losing it did not cover what she had done. This time, Libby girl, she told herself, you've really crossed over into the dark side and closed the door behind you.

'I noticed you.'

Her startled gaze flew to his face. Of all the things she had imagined him saying in response to her slightly insane tirade, this had not featured.

Her eyes connected with his smouldering, mesmeric stare and Libby stopped breathing.

Lust licked through her body like an out-of-control forest fire, hardening her nipples to painful prominence.

She expelled a long shuddering sigh and lifted her chin, blocking the relentless flow of steamy images her treacherous mind was forming. The effort required to achieve this made beads of sweat break out along her upper lip.

'Waiting for me to fall flat on my face, I suppose.'

'I thought you handled yourself pretty well in there.'

Again his response was not what she had expected. 'And in there—I have to say I don't appreciate your sense of humour. Did you ever have any intention of giving me an internship?'

'You expect me to treat you any differently from other interns? You require preferential treatment?'

Libby loosed an incredulous laugh. 'Oh, sure, I'm sure you get all your interns to pour coffee.' Hating the hurt quiver in her voice, she bit down hard on her lower lip, trapping the weak sob that ached for release in her throat.

Rafael felt horror as he watched her eyes fill with tears, but he refused to soften his attitude. No doubt her big blue eyes and tears had been making people soften her path all her life, but he was not falling into that pattern.

'Not all.'

His attitude stoked her fury. 'Not any!' she contended angrily.

'Believe it or not, it's true. You were not singled out for special treatment. You remember Callum, the man with me that you spoke to?' *Smiled at.*

Libby nodded.

Rafael forced the fists clenched at his sides to unclench. 'He was an intern—his first day was spent in the post room.'

Libby stared, not sure if she believed him.

'This place works as a team. Respect for what other people do is essential. I appreciate and respect what everyone here does but I have swept roads and washed windows.

'Many of the people who come here from university have not taken that route. Some, not all, have led privileged lives,' he said, looking at her hard. 'They arrive with an over-inflated opinion of their place in the scheme of things and sometimes a lack of respect for people lower down the ranks than them.'

'And you make them serve coffee.'

'Amongst other things.'

'So this was some sort of test?' Had she passed?

He arched a brow. 'You could look at it that way.'

'So this is for real? You are giving me a chance to help my family.' She remembered she had called him a bastard and paled.

'Your father will receive information from my legal department telling him that the closure has been put on hold while the figures are re-examined.'

'So it all depends on me.'

'Yes.'

'So no pressure, then.' She glanced up at him. 'You don't think I can do it, do you?'

His brilliant eyes scanned her face. 'Forget what I think...what do you think?'

Libby's chin lifted and she nodded. 'I think I'll be the best intern you've ever had.'

CHAPTER TEN

WHILE she was not the best, during her first week Libby Marchant proved to be *different*.

Far from behaving like the spoilt prima donna he had once accused her of being, she had, according to the reports he had received, shown a willingness to throw herself with enthusiasm into everything requested of her.

He could find no fault with her work ethic and general keenness; it was the more personal quirky touches that he had doubts about. He liked the office environment to be an emotion-free zone, he expected his employees to leave their problems at home and, had the question ever arisen, he would have felt the same about home baking.

The muffin situation was getting seriously out of hand. He could barely walk past a desk without seeing some garishly decorated home-baked goodies on display. He was struggling to keep an open mind on the subject, though he suspected a baked-goods ban would not go down well so while it only affected personal waistlines he was holding fire.

The soccer situation was not so innocent. Could anything be innocent when young testosterone-fuelled sportsmen were involved? Rafael had been startled and not entirely pleased to learn only that morning that his new intern had been adopted as the mascot of the firm's five-a-side soccer team after her appearance on the touchline had coincided with their first ever win.

The team, which had in his opinion more testosterone than talent in its ranks, apparently now called her their lucky charm. He had no doubt they called her other things in the changing rooms. Did she even realise she had made herself the butt of sexist jokes and ribaldry?

Arriving on the Monday of her second week, Libby received a summons to Rafael's office.

Standing in the outer office, this time by invitation, she was directed to a chair by Rafael's gorgeous blonde PA. Opinion in the building was divided on whether her relationship with their boss extended as far as the bedroom.

Libby waited and felt like a naughty schoolgirl summoned to the headmaster's office.

Or as her family would have said—that *monster's* office. She supposed there would never have been a good time to tell them, but the strength of their reaction when she had come clean the previous night had shocked her; so, if she was honest with herself, had the degree to which her own view of the situation had shifted.

She leaned back in her seat as selected highlights of the conversation drifted through her head.

She had not entered into the discussion over the dinner table concerning the rather unexpected reprieve. Her father, happily but rather unrealistically predicting that Rafael Alejandro would come to him for advice any day now, had contended that the Spaniard had realised he had made a mistake.

'He doesn't have the experience, just not the man to fill Aldo's shoes, but they were big shoes.'

Libby, listening, had had to bite her tongue to stop herself revealing the truth. A week ago she might have agreed, but now it felt quite wrong that all the blame should be laid at Rafael's door.

'I'd thought of taking a trip to the races on Monday.'

'Excellent idea—we could all go,' Kate Marchant had approved. 'It would take your mind off things.'

Libby had felt guilty to find herself thinking that her father was too good at taking his mind off things.

'How about you, Libby? I could speak to Mike about giving you a day off.'

'No.'

'Oh, Mike won't mind,' her dad had promised, patting her hand.

'I handed in my notice last week.' It was a risk

but for once in her life Libby wanted to work without a safety net.

Her parents had stared at her. 'But why?' they had asked in unison, dismayed but not at that stage angry—the anger had come later.

'Actually I have another job…well, internship really, but—'

'Well, that's excellent. Well done, darling, but why on earth didn't you tell us?'

'I'm working for Rafael Alejandro—not personally, obviously.'

'You're not serious!'

'Blood pressure, darling,' Kate Marchant had warned. 'It's just a joke—tell him, Libby…'

'It's true. I was working there all last week.'

From that point things had got extremely heated, her father had accused her of disloyalty and called her a silly little girl, her mother had cried.

'But this experience could get me a good job.' Still unwilling to raise false hopes, she had refrained from telling them the benefit her internship could bring their way.

'You have a good job,' her father had protested.

'Dad, I cover dog shows. I'm bored.'

Her dad had given a contemptuous snort. 'Bored! Since when?'

Since always, she had realised with a sense of shock.

'He'll see you now.'

The blonde PA's voice jolted Libby back to the present.

'Thank you.' Libby took a deep breath and accepted the invitation to enter the inner sanctum.

Last time he carried me.

The thought made her stumble, but luckily her gracelessness went unnoticed—Rafael wasn't looking.

He didn't even glance up. She waited, shifting her weight from one foot to the other, her resentment and nervousness growing with each passing second that he continued to study the paper set on the desk before him.

It seemed ironic now that she had worried about sexual harassment. Far from his harassing her, the only time their paths had crossed since that first day Libby had been left with a tentative smile on her face feeling stupid as Rafael had blanked her totally.

Clearly his egalitarian rules had exceptions.

Libby told herself she didn't *want* him to notice her; she didn't want to notice him, not that way, but she couldn't help it.

On that occasion it had taken Libby's tumultuous pulse ten minutes to return to anything approaching normal.

Libby stared at the dark hair curling into his strong neck and, feeling things start to shift and tighten deep inside, thought what was she doing.

'This week you will be shadowing...' Rafael paused and lifted his head.

He saw her standing hands folded primly in front of her, her luscious body looking the total opposite of prim, looking in fact luscious, and he forgot what he was saying as lust slammed through his body with a force that pushed him back into his seat.

'You?'

Rafael pushed away the image of her lying

across his desk, her short skirt around her waist, and cleared his throat.

Following him around all day, sitting within feet of him! He did not trust himself to move the other side of the desk. 'No, not me.'

'Good...' She met his eyes and blushed. 'That is, I'm sure you're too important to bother with interns.' She sounded like a total sycophant on board the Rafael worshipping express with everyone else here. 'I meant...'

It was Rafael's deep voice that stopped her digging herself any deeper. 'One intern bothers me a lot.'

Libby swallowed. 'I...they do?' He'd said she'd know when he asked her, but she didn't—was this it?

His hot hungry eyes brushed hers for a split second before his lashes swept downwards.

Rafael, pretending he hadn't heard her choked little gasp, directed his gaze at the paper before him. 'Gretchen will fill you in with the details.'

Libby, hurt by the dismissal, confused by the mixed messages he was sending and eaten up by guilt because she was so fatally attracted to a man who had done so much damage to her family, turned slowly.

Rafael watched her walk away, her slender back straight, her head held high. He waited for the door to close before he dragged a hand through his hair and groaned.

He could have had her here and now on the desk… His head fell back; he was a fool.

His rule was not to mix business and his private life; he had delivered a lecture on the evils of sexual harassment to every member of the football team, but when principles were this painful wasn't it time to change the rules?

He wasn't just her boss, though; he held the fate of her family in his hands. Would she dare say no? He grinned and thought she would dare say anything, but would that doubt remain—would it sour any future relationship?

An expression of shock spread across his lean face—future and relationship were two words he never used in connection with a woman.

Following her now would be admitting that this

woman had got so deep under his skin that he couldn't wait three weeks.

He needed a cooling-off period.

He pressed the intercom and barked, 'I will be going to Rio—arrange it.'

Rafael's arrival mid-afternoon a week later at the London headquarters office coincided with the exit from the building of the regional manager, who did a double take when he saw Rafael.

Simon Smith rushed over. 'Is there a problem?' he asked, looking concerned.

Rafael took the hand extended towards him in a firm grip; his problem, the one that had brought him back five days ahead of schedule, was five feet five and red-headed.

The two men shook hands. 'Your family is well?' Rafael, not normally someone who felt the need to fill a silence when he had nothing to say, heard himself murmur the pleasantry.

To cover his own unacknowledged embarrassment?

The possibility did not improve his frame of

mind. He could rationalise as much as he liked—nothing would alter the fact he was responding to his hormones with all the restraint of an adolescent.

There was a shade of puzzlement behind the older man's smile as he responded. 'Very well, thank you, although James is—' He stopped, awkwardness creeping into his manner as he added with a laugh, 'I'm sure you don't want to know about his latest—'

The indent between Rafael's brows deepened. '*James...?* Is he not the one who celebrated his twenty-first birthday at Christmas?'

Simon looked momentarily startled. He was amazed that his boss recalled he had children, let alone that he knew the age of his eldest. 'You know how it is with children. No matter how old they are you still worry—' He gave a shrug, regretting his comment. His employer's opinion on the subject of professionalism and bringing personal problems into the workplace was well known.

'No, I do not know,' Rafael admitted shortly.

How could he? There had been no father figure in his life to worry about his choices or to guide him, not that Rafael felt the loss of something he had never had. He preferred to concentrate on the positive benefits he had gained from his unconventional upbringing.

His ability to make a decision and live with the consequences, good or bad, came from those years. Would a nuclear family have given him the sort of self-reliance that had been the bedrock of his success, Rafael doubted it.

Had his early years been different, would he have one day had a photo of his son in his graduation gown on his desk like Simon? Rafael did not know and there was no gain in speculating, he reminded himself. A man lived with what was and not what might have been, and fatherhood was not a role he had ever considered for himself.

Would it happen? He enjoyed being a free agent. Some people might consider him selfish but to Rafael's mind it would be more selfish to take on a role that you were patently unsuited to.

And scared of.

Rafael pushed away the silent addition. It was not a matter of fear, it was a matter of practicality and personal preference. Of course, if things had been different he supposed it was possible he might have felt it his duty to continue the name of an ancient family. As it was he owed no loyalty to the family who had rejected him.

That rejection had freed him to do as he wished and he did not wish to spend his life constantly in the middle of some sort of domestic crisis like Simon here.

How did someone like Simon, with a challenging job and a large family, manage to cope with the various demands on his time?

It would not do for him. Rafael had always been scrupulous about keeping his own personal life separate from business, and his life had balance.

Or it had had!

'There is no problem,' Rafael lied smoothly. 'Things moved faster than anticipated and Lucas had things under control.'

Just as well someone did!

Ironically his team and the opposition had assumed that his lack of interest was some sort of clever mind game to throw the opposition off their game and it had.

He'd been lucky this time, but Rafael knew that luck and his reputation wouldn't save him another time. Reputations could be lost overnight; all it took was a few bad decisions for the market to lose confidence.

Rafael knew he could not afford to lose his edge. He couldn't carry on struggling to concentrate because he was wondering what Libby was doing, if she was waiting anxiously for his return, if she was smiling at other men…

His brain had been hijacked by his temporary intern.

This preoccupation was alien to him. His ability to compartmentalise the disparate aspects of his life had always been a given for Rafael. To have that ability desert him, to find his mind wandering and his thoughts filled exclusively with one face, had made him wonder if he was losing it.

The sobering thought had focused him and it

had been with relief he had realised he wasn't losing anything—he just wasn't getting it!

This wasn't about losing his edge, it was about sex. He was a man with healthy appetites, not accustomed to putting any effort into getting the object of his interest into bed.

Despite his notorious reputation, Rafael was the one normally being pursued, and it had always been that way. Since he had entered adolescence women had been attracted to him.

He had told himself that the chase would be good for his jaded appetite, give him time to savour the pleasure of her eventual surrender.

But the pleasure of the chase was one thing, and this, this hunger gnawing away at him like acid, was not pleasure, it was torture!

He was not a naturally patient man, so why go against type now? He had finally realised the error of being too patient, of overcomplicating the situation; the solution was simple—he wanted her and she wanted him. It was time to bring the situation to a conclusion and get back to normality.

He had never been in a relationship for longer

than a few weeks before. How long would it take for the fascination to fade, for the hunger to be sated?

Libby had enjoyed her second week. Rob Monroe, a fatherly Scottish man with a dry sense of humour, had greeted her warmly.

'Rafael wants you to experience as many aspects of the business as possible during your time with us.'

'I'll do my best,' Libby promised, thinking, This is where it really starts. She found herself excited by the prospect.

It was later that day when, unable to help herself, she awkwardly introduced the subject that had been on her mind all morning. 'Mr Alejandro, does he…will he be…*around*…much this week?'

If she got told it was none of her business, fair enough. To Libby's way of thinking being put in her place was infinitely preferable to glancing over her shoulder every two seconds. If he was going to pop up she wanted to be forewarned.

'Rafael is out of the country.'

'He is?' Conscious that her reaction to this news

was worryingly ambiguous, she concentrated on the relief section, wisely not delving deeper into the tiny flash of something resembling anticlimax.

'I thought you'd know.'

Libby shook her head. 'Me? Why should I…?'

The older man had looked uncomfortable. 'Well, you and he are…friends?'

For friends Libby read lovers. The heat rushed to her face—so the half of the company who didn't think the lovely Gretchen was sleeping with him thought she was.

Libby knew her cheeks were burning but she kept her glance steady as she looked the older man directly in the eyes. 'Why would you think that?'

There was a pause before he smiled and nodded his head. 'My mistake. Rafael will be out of the country for most of the next two weeks.'

Libby received this information in silence. Good news obviously, which begged the worrying question why she experienced a sinking sensation that strongly resembled anticlimax.

'As you know…' He paused and added, 'Or

maybe not, he has extensive interests in South America.'

Libby could only hope that Rob Monroe shared his *mistake* with others. She was never sure if he had, but the attitude of other people she encountered in the building had for the most part been positive—until today, when she arrived to the news that her mentor was ill, nothing more dramatic than the flu but enough to keep him at home for the rest of the week.

Deputising for him was his junior, a stylish brunette in her mid thirties. The previous week Libby had reached the point where, against all expectation, she was actually looking forward to arriving at work.

She was already dreading tomorrow. Her new mentor performed her task with obvious reluctance, ignoring Libby most of the time and only introducing her to anyone when pointedly asked.

Libby had stood around feeling uncomfortably like a spare part. Opening her mouth triggered an exaggerated sequence of eye rolling from the older woman, followed by a tart reminder that she was there in a supernumerary capacity to observe, not participate.

Libby, who knew when she was beat, had eventually stopped opening her mouth. Wasting all this valuable learning time was really frustrating, but what choice did she have? It was true—she was meant to observe, not participate.

Libby, determined to prove herself capable to spite Rafael, just hoped that Rob Monroe would be well soon.

Her reluctant mentor hadn't even bothered to keep up the pretence of letting Libby trail after her—instead after lunch she planted a stack of papers on her desk and asked for an analysis, her expression suggesting that she did not anticipate getting it.

It had taken Libby most of the afternoon to figure out what she was meant to produce an analysis on, but, determined to prove the woman wrong if it killed her, she ploughed on. By four she had realised it might not kill her but it was going to give her one hell of a headache. The fact she had skipped breakfast and not yet made it to lunch had probably not helped.

Hoping to head off the familiar symptoms, she headed out into the corridor, intending to get a glass of iced water to help wash down her migraine medication.

It was there, with a hand pressed to her throbbing head, that Libby, her thoughts still on the figures revolving in her head, almost ploughed straight into Jake Wylie, the lawyer that Susie had set her up with in New York the previous month. His surprise when he recognised her was equal to her own.

'Now this is what I call fate,' he said after she'd given a brief and strictly expurgated reason for her presence.

Not fate, but it was really good to see a familiar face in an environment where she felt like a fish out of water—there had been moments today when she'd felt so isolated and alone that she'd found herself anticipating, and not in a totally negative way, turning around and seeing Rafael standing there!

They began to chat. Jake was a very good listener and, unlike Rafael, you could take what he said at face value. There were no sinister undertones to worry about—or sexual attraction—which made him very easy to relax around.

Having worked through her lunch break, Libby, who was in desperate need of a coffee, invited Jake to join her. She was genuinely delighted when he accepted.

She was midway through pouring Jake a coffee when her mobile rang. Libby smiled an apology and lifted it to her ear and heard her brother's voice.

'How is—?'

Her brother cut across her. 'Is it true?'

Her parents had told her they were not going to tell her brother because he had enough on his plate, adding that they were hoping she had come to her senses before then. Clearly they had decided that with the baby home and Meg fully recovered his plate was clear enough now.

'Yes, I'm working for Rafael Alejandro, but there are reasons—'

'I'm not interested in reasons, Libby, the only thing I'm interested in hearing you say is you're walking out of that building.'

'I can't say that.'

'Have you any idea how upset Mum is? I can't believe how selfish you're being.'

Libby felt her eyes fill with tears. 'Maybe I am.' It was a question she had asked herself more than once—ever since she had realised that she was no longer doing this just for her family: she was doing it for herself.

She winced as the sound of the phone slamming into the cradle vibrated down the line.

'Are you all right?'

Libby caught her trembling lower lip between her teeth and shook her head. 'Family stuff.' She stopped, pressing a hand to her mouth as her voice was suspended by tears.

She gave a mortified sniff and shook her head in apology.

Jake's expression became instantly sympathetic. 'Don't worry—the things I could tell you about my family.' And he proceeded to do just that. Libby had no idea if the story of a disastrous Thanksgiving family dinner was real, but it made her laugh.

'Thank you and sorry about the waterworks.'

The handsome American gave a smile that crinkled his eyes and touched her shoulder. 'I have four sisters and an ex-wife. I know all about crying. Don't mind me, let it out,' he advised, giving her shoulder a friendly squeeze.

The show of sympathy brought a fresh rush of moisture to her eyes. Libby blinked, swallowing past the aching emotional stricture in her throat as she firmed her shoulders.

He meant well, of course, but she had no intention of taking Jake's advice. If she let go, if for one moment she lowered her defences and let the emotions she had walled up over the past few weeks loose, the resulting torrent would not be pretty.

'You're kind.' She scanned his face, thinking, And good-looking and smart. Why, she wondered, couldn't I have been attracted to this nice man and not—? Libby shook her head and pushed the thought aside. There were some realities she was not ready to admit even to herself just yet.

Not ever!

Jake watched as she reached for a tissue from the box on the desk; he pushed it closer. 'A kind lawyer, two words that in my experience rarely precede women ripping my clothes off…?'

Libby shook her head and gave an apologetic smile. 'I'm not really looking for—' She broke off awkwardly.

The American gave a philosophical shrug. 'I thought so but no harm in trying, and watch out—you know what they say?'

Libby shook her head.

'You always find it when you're not looking.' He gave a frown and added, 'Or was that it finds you?

'How do you feel about dinner anyway? I'm in town for the rest of the week. I promise not to produce any more homespun wisdom and you could tell me what the legendary Rafael Alejandro is like in real life.'

'Rafael Alejandro!'

Libby inhaled deeply through flared nostrils. She had developed an almost Pavlovian response to that name. Hear or think it—which she did more frequently than she liked to admit—and she experienced a dramatic hormone rush followed by an equally strong period of self-loathing.

It was a name that pressed more buttons than Libby could count!

She barely registered Jake's startled expression when a bitter laugh was wrenched from her lips.

'I can tell you that now. He's an arrogant, self-opinionated, conceited, unscrupulous, devious—' Breathing hard, she brought her short tirade to an abrupt halt.

Yes, Libby, that *really* came across as a disinterested analysis.

Jake let out a silent whistle. 'Wow. I take it I'm not talking to a fan.'

CHAPTER ELEVEN

LIBBY, appalled and embarrassed by her outburst, struggled for composure. 'He is not a man who inspires mild feelings,' she admitted with a little laugh.

'Am I interrupting?'

Libby loosed a gasp and turned her head jerkily, her complexion going through several dramatically rapid shade changes before she faced the man framed in the doorway, her eyes wide and horror-filled in a face that was porcelain pale.

Rafael Alejandro, his face a stony mask, levered his lean length from the doorframe, channelling dark, mean and brooding from every perfect, arrogant pore as he tipped his dark head, displayed a perfect set of white teeth and divided his nasty sardonic smile between her and Jake.

Her outburst replaying in her head—he had

obviously heard every word—Libby bit her lip to restrain the groan that rose in her throat, utterly helpless to control the rush of liquid heat that surged through her body.

She watched as he levered his shoulder off the doorframe and straightened up to his full impressive height before sauntering into the room with the feline grace of a jungle cat.

'I was just—'

'Yes, I heard.'

Libby swallowed, her cheeks flaming, and lowered her gaze, struggling to regain a semblance of control. She had meant every word she had said in her no-holds-barred summary of his character; her only inaccuracy lay in omission.

You could not describe Rafael Alejandro without mentioning the trivial detail that he was arguably—no argument in Libby's mind—the most incredible-looking man on the planet. But no description of his well-built body, chiselled features and sexy mouth could articulate the force field of arrogant, raw sexuality he projected.

It was something a person had to feel to appreciate. Libby was feeling it now, feeling it from her scalp to her toes.

She wondered if she was having a heart attack.

'I am intruding?' His questioning glance slid past Libby and to the man beside her.

Libby missed the social cue. 'No…yes…that is…' Libby stopped. Forced onto the offensive by sheer embarrassment, she snapped crankily, 'What are you doing here?'

Rafael raised a brow and Libby bit her lip, feeling a total idiot.

'That is, this is a surprise. Nobody told me you were coming.'

'I had no idea I was meant to inform you.'

Jake, who had been silent, stepped in to fill the awkward silence. 'Jake Wylie…'

For an awful moment Libby thought that Rafael was not going to take the hand extended to him.

The contact was brief. After subjecting him to a stare that made the ice cap look warm and cosily benevolent by contrast Rafael ignored the other man totally and turned his attention to Libby.

'Right, well, I must be going. It was very nice to

meet you and it was lovely to catch up, Libby…'
Jake threw her an apologetic look.

There was a silence after the door closed behind
Jake, broken eventually by Rafael.

'You have been putting your time to good use,
I see. I am all for thinking outside the box, but I
think you might have the wrong idea about what
skills are required when running a light manufacturing company.' His lips curled into an expressive sneer of disdain.

The smiling insult drew a gasp from Libby.
'That was totally uncalled for!'

'In this building I do not receive lessons on
manners, I deliver them!' The stinging rebuke
brought a fresh rush of anger to her cheeks.

'And actually I think that under the circumstances I was admirably restrained. You are meant
to be shadowing Rob. Instead I find you making
out with someone on your desk. I'm assuming
you have worked your way through the football
team.'

'I was not on my desk…or making out,' she

added hastily. 'And Mr Monroe...Rob...he is sick.' She shook her head and added, *'Football team?'*

'Why was I not told?'

'How should I know?'

A nerve ticked along Rafael's jaw. 'Who is responsible for giving you this junk?' He picked up the file on top of the pile and waved it towards her.

Libby deflected the question. 'Why—are you going to bully her too?' She might not like the woman, but she would not put her worst enemy in Rafael Alejandro's firing line.

He stared at her face, betraying little beyond blank incredulity. *'Bully?'*

She lifted her chin another defiant inch and met the blaze of his golden stare head-on. 'You heard me.'

She saw something dark and dangerous flare in Rafael's mesmeric eyes and swallowed, moistening her suddenly dry lips with the tip of her tongue.

'Please go on, you fascinate me.' At one level

Libby did know that this was probably the worst advice in the world to take. But she was way past taking the sensible option. Besides, this situation was past fixing by grovelling. It was obvious she'd already totally blown whatever chance she had of saving her father from financial ruin, so why hold back?

What was the worst he could do?

Libby's thoughts veered away from the question.

'You know what my definition of a bully is?'

Rafael's dark brows twitched into an interrogative dark line above his hawkish nose as he folded his arms across his chest, his eyes trained on her heaving bosom, and he murmured, 'I feel sure you are going to tell me.'

Libby's chin lifted. 'A bully is someone who browbeats, humiliates and harasses someone else who is in no position to respond.'

With each successive indictment the skin pulled tighter across the fabulous bones of his face. Libby couldn't drag her eyes from the frenetic nerve pumping away like a time bomb in his lean cheek.

'They only pick on people who can't or won't fight back!'

Rafael ground his teeth. 'Nothing,' he gritted, 'would have pleased me more than if your *friend* had taken a swing at me.'

'My friend is a gentleman, but I might punch you myself! In fact I should. I'd love to know what you said to make half the damned building think that I'm only here because we're…' The hint of angry colour in her cheeks deepened to a mortified scarlet as Libby shook her head. 'It doesn't matter.'

Rafael put the file down and began to flick through the rest of the paperwork on her desk. A few files down he began to frown. 'What doesn't matter?' Having reached the bottom of the stack, he turned his gaze on Libby and arched a questioning brow.

Libby sighed and began to wish she'd never introduced the subject.

'They think we're sleeping together.'

The sardonic humour in his eyes vanished as a

heavy frown settled on his sternly beautiful features. 'Who has said this to you?'

'Nobody has said anything, but I can see that's what they're thinking.'

Rafael picked up an empty paper cup from the desk, crushed it between his fingers before lobbing it casually into the waste-paper bin several feet away. 'You are paranoid.'

Libby clenched her teeth; his accented drawl really got under her skin. 'I am not paranoid!'

'And fearful of gossip.'

Libby's chin went up. 'I'm not afraid of gossip.'

'Just afraid your lover will think you're sleeping with another man.'

Libby responded to the goad without thinking. 'Jake is not my lover.'

A slow smile spread across his lean face. 'Good, it is not my habit to share my women.'

Breathing through the shameful stab of lust low in her belly, Libby struggled to look amused

'Do you know how ridiculous that sounds?' It *should*, so why didn't it? 'I know it's your life's mission to put the cool in Neanderthal but really…

my woman?' On the receiving end of another powerful kick of lust, she added crankily, 'And even if I was it would hardly make me feel special, would it, to be one amongst so many? What… what are you smiling at?' she demanded, viewing the sudden change in his expression with suspicion.

'I too have been very frustrated,' he admitted bluntly.

The colour rushed to her face as Libby shook her head in denial—if only it were so easy to deny the illicit thrill that had edged the tingling sensation inside past uncomfortable and deeply into painful territory. 'You're deluded. Do you *honestly* think that every woman you have met casually sits at her desk lusting after you?' Maybe not everyone but Libby was willing to bet there were quite a few.

'We did not meet casually. You almost killed me.'

'And you're never going to let me forget it!'

If only she could let herself. Her brain had recorded and stored every second of the time she had spent with him along with a few that hadn't happened—*yet!*

Libby's gasp of horror locked painfully in her aching throat; her eyelashes lowered in a protective sweep. The moment she started acting as though this was inevitable she was in trouble.

'Will you stop staring at your shoes and look at me?'

'No.'

Rafael's lips curved into a reluctant smile. 'You sound like a sulky five-year-old. Look,' he said, dragging a hand through his hair as he took a step closer. 'Neither of us chose for this to happen but it has.'

Libby shook her head. 'Nothing has happened.'

Rafael, not a man inclined to wrap things up with pretty words, opened his mouth fully expecting to hear himself say something along the lines of, I want to have sex with you, with the option of throwing in the additional information of the imminent risk to his sanity if he didn't.

Instead he heard the sentence, 'I would like to get to know you better,' come out of his mouth.

She did look at him then. The astonishment on her face did not even begin to approach the shock he was feeling, but then she did not know that he had just said something he had never even thought, let alone voiced, in his life.

The wheels of Rafael's mind began to turn. For whatever reason he had given voice to subconscious thoughts he would have been more comfortable ignoring, but they were out there now.

He had not so much actively avoided emotional entanglements as not felt the need to become involved. He was self-sufficient and not into sharing himself with others.

Without him even realising it, his interest in a woman had for the first time in his life gone past the physical. Not only had Libby aroused a primal hunger that refused to subside, she had somehow got into his head.

'Because you're interested in my mind and not my body.'

Rafael cut her an impatient look. 'And my body does nothing for you at all, I suppose.' He flicked the button on his jacket with one finger, a slow mocking smile curving his lips as he held his hands wide.

A distracted expression drifted across Libby's face as she was unable to refuse the unspoken invitation in his actions—her first mistake. The next was to allow herself to imagine what lay beneath the silk shirt he wore, to allow the image of hard satiny skin and taut muscle to form in her head, an image so strong, so tactile, that it seemed more real to her than the pain she felt as her teeth dug into the soft flesh of her lower lip.

Libby felt things twist and tighten low in her belly, her appreciation sliding seamlessly from the aesthetic into primitive fascination.

The effort of dragging her eyes away brought a sheen of moisture to her smooth brow. She was horrified. She had never felt this level of fascination for a man's body before. She was mad with herself for being so weak and with him for being so damned sure of himself.

So damned unbelievably gorgeous.

'You don't like what you see.'

'I see a man who has serious self-esteem issues.'

Despite the frustration that was stretching his frayed control to the limit, the sarcastic sally drew a laugh from Rafael.

'Look, the fact is we have chemistry.' A week to think about little else and that is the best you can come up with, Rafael? *Chemistry!*

Chemistry was a pathetically inadequate word hardly covering the wanting that had filled his every waking moment since he had laid eyes on her. The primitive power of the reaction she evoked in him was like nothing he had ever experienced.

'You know I'm attracted to you.'

Libby turned her head, ashamed of the flutter of excitement low in her belly.

'And don't pretend that knowledge does not excite you.'

'We may have…*chemistry,*' she admitted the charge, enunciating the word with distaste. 'But I also have a brain.' She saw no point in mentioning the fact it was not functioning at that moment. 'Nothing is ever going to happen between us. Even if I wanted it to I couldn't…'

'Why?'

'You're not serious!' She studied his chiselled patrician features with an expression of sheer incredulity.

'I see nothing stopping us enjoying a sexual relationship.'

Libby forced a laugh and struggled to maintain a veneer of calm, conscious as she did so of how fragile it was. 'Me not wanting to sleep with you?'

He gave a shrug of acknowledgement. 'If it were true, yes, it would.'

Their glances locked; it was Libby who looked away from his steady gaze first. 'Even if I was into casual sex I couldn't go to bed with a man who my family believes is responsible for...' She stopped and gave a twisted smile. 'Actually it would be easier to say what my family don't think you're responsible for.' It had been simpler when she had shared their feelings.

'I am not asking your family to have sex with me.'

Libby controlled the childish urge to stamp her foot—just. 'It would be sleeping with the enemy!'

His inability to grasp the obvious was frustrating—almost as frustrating as looking at his mouth and not being able to kiss him. 'I couldn't do that to them, so short of having a secret affair... It's bad enough the way they look at me now,' she reflected with sigh. 'Imagine if...' She gave a shudder at the thought of how betrayed they'd feel. 'I'd die if it came out!' And things like that inevitably did.

Rafael searched her face. She seemed utterly oblivious to the fact that she had offered him any offence.

It was not as though he wanted to advertise details of his personal life on a billboard, but he had never before encountered a woman who announced that she would be ashamed to have it known she shared his bed.

'What have you told your family?'

'Some but not all,' she admitted. 'They don't know that you might not close the firm.'

A look of amazement chased across the surface of his lean face. 'They don't know?'

She shook her head. '*Maybe* they'd be all right

with it, but the truth is I honestly don't know how they'd react, not after the way they reacted when I said I'd handed in my notice to work for you.'

A look of shock crossed his face. 'You handed in your notice?'

She nodded. 'I'm serious about this.' She looked at him and thought uneasily, Are you? 'It didn't seem worth telling them everything when I might blow it anyway.'

'But you are trying to save them.'

'They might not see it that way.'

'So you lied to them.'

'That's the thing with lies and half-truths— once you start it is difficult to stop.' She finished speaking when the anger in his eyes brought her frowning scrutiny to his face.

For a man who was very good at hiding his feelings, he was not hiding them now. Libby did not have to look very closely to see that he was inexplicably angry—very angry.

'However, relax. I am not about to be any woman's dirty little secret, so consider the subject of our hypothetical affair closed.'

The pressure was off, she ought to be happy—of course she wasn't. Perversely the moment the offer was retracted, almost before the door had closed behind him, Libby realised how much she had wanted to say yes, wanted to be persuaded to throw caution to the winds and be selfishly reckless.

CHAPTER TWELVE

LIBBY slipped on her trainers and popped her heels in her bag.

She had the timing down to a fine art and, as she had learnt, unforeseen delays could mean she missed her connection and got home even later.

The unforeseen delay this evening was Rafael's tall blonde PA stroke mistress. On two occasions since she had started here Libby had caught glimpses of her outside the office. She wasn't easy to miss; each time she had dodged her. It was not an acquaintance she felt eager to renew!

This time she did not have the option of running away. She stumbled into her and knocked the oversized designer bag the blonde was carrying out of her hands.

The contents spilled out across the corridor.

'I'm so sorry,' Libby mumbled, dropping to her knees to gather them up.

'No problem,' Gretchen said, opening her bag to allow Libby to drop the retrieved items back in. 'No, the lipstick goes in the compartment and the tissues…great.'

The smile, all warmth and teeth, made Libby blink.

'I've been hoping to get a chance to talk to you outside the office,' the girl continued. 'I know that the first time we met, you must have thought I was rude or barking, which as you now know I am—well, the barking bit anyhow.' She looked at Libby's face and laughed. 'You don't have the faintest idea what I'm talking about, do you?'

Libby shook her head, struggling to reconcile her mental image of the statuesque blonde who had blanked her with this warm and effervescent woman.

'I thought the grapevine would have filled you in, the general weirdness you witnessed at the crash scene, and I'm sorry I didn't explain at the time. Poor you—that was my OCD kicking in, two of my worst nightmares being lateness and dirt. Most of the time I'm fairly normal.'

Libby, not quite sure how to respond to this confidence, mumbled an embarrassed. 'Oh, I'm sorry.'

'Oh, don't be, you wouldn't believe how much better I am. That therapist that Rafael made me go to, he's just—' She shook her head. 'But enough about me. I'm really glad I bumped into you. I heard about earlier.'

Libby's stomach took a sickening lurch. Did the entire building know or had Rafael not posted the events online yet?

The tall blonde patted her hand. 'Don't worry, you weren't being singled out for special attention.'

'Good to know.' Did this mean he propositioned all staff or just the female ones? Libby wondered, biting back a bubble of hysterical laughter.

'He's got this thing about not bringing personal stuff into work, and there's a zero-tolerance policy on office romances. It was just bad luck he walked in and saw you with your boyfriend.'

'He wasn't my boyfriend.'

'Really?' She arched a brow. 'Not like Rafael

to jump to conclusions, but you wouldn't believe the mood he was in this evening. I hope he didn't upset you too much. Remember, it's not just you— he's even got cranky with me in the past when I've taken calls from my partner, Cara, which is taking it too far.'

'Cara, nice name.' The penny clicked and Libby's eyes flew wide. 'A girl, you're...oh, no, I'm sorry.'

'Don't worry,' the other girl said with a serene laugh as Libby blushed. 'I get a lot of that. Some people even think that Rafael and me are an item.'

'Amazing!' Libby breathed faintly.

'I sometimes think he only gave me the job in the first place because there was no chance of me falling for him. Well, you've seen him, so I don't have to tell you how many girls get crushes on him.'

'No...yes, you do have to tell me. I don't find him at all attractive.' Libby closed her eyes and thought, Please let me die now!

'You're not...?'

Libby blushed again and thought, Could I seem

more provincial. 'No, I'm not.' Did the women of the world really fall into two categories: those in love with Rafael and those who were gay?

'Not that I have a problem. I like men, just not *that* man…he…' Judging it was about time she stopped digging the hole she was standing in, she glanced at her watch and said she'd miss her train if she didn't run.

As she legged it down the corridor she heard Gretchen yell after her. 'Oh, by the way, I love muffins and brownies…'

Actually she would probably miss the train anyway.

Outside Libby hunched her shoulders inside her thin coat. The temperature had dropped ten degrees since that morning and the wind was biting. She glanced at her watch and grimaced as she broke into a trot; she didn't hear the car until it stopped right beside her.

Rafael leaned across and opened the passenger door. Libby, her heart pounding like a sledgehammer inside her ribcage, barely noticed as the door swung against her legs.

'I'm in a hurry. My train—'

Rafael acted as though she hadn't spoken. 'Get in.'

To her shame Libby found herself obeying the terse direction without even putting up a token protest. Telling herself as she slid into the leather seat that it was because someone might see her.

'How long will it take you to get home on the train?'

'It depends if the train's on time,' she said, thinking, Why are we having this conversation? 'And if I catch the first connection, not the—'

Rafael cut through her calculations. 'I can get you home earlier,' he announced confidently.

'You could,' she agreed, suddenly breathless. 'But why should you?'

'I am a considerate guy?'

Libby didn't respond to the dry humour in his voice, or register that it was not echoed in the driven expression glowing in his deep-set eyes, she was too busy with basic stuff like breathing.

Her imagination was running riot. Was he about to repeat his earlier proposition?

The possibility made her throat grow dry. Was this a chance to change her mind, to make a total fool of herself?

Both maybe?

He arched a brow and studied her tense face. The inner fire he always sensed tantalisingly beneath that cool façade seemed closer to the surface as his glance connected with her wide blue eyes.

'No?' Then, impatience creeping into his manner, he added, 'Does it matter why? The fact is I am willing to deliver you safely home, guarantee you get there when you should.'

'I'm hearing a but.' She was also hearing bells, which she was studiously ignoring.

'Fasten your seat belt.' He fastened his own and flashed an irritated look her way. 'If I stay here much longer I'll get a ticket. There is no but.' He scanned her face, reading the scepticism and seeing the dark shadows under her eyes, the lines of strain etched in the skin around her mouth.

While he was not directly responsible for putting them there, he had to struggle to keep his protective instincts in check.

Something about this woman seemed to exaggerate all his emotional responses. One second he wanted to protect her from a light wind, the next he wanted to throttle her. The desire to fling her down and slide deep into her warm body was pretty much a constant.

He was basing his present actions on the assumption that once he had satisfied the latter of these impulses his emotional equilibrium would return to normal.

'There will even be time for you to have some supper with me.' She looked as if she needed feeding.

'I'm not hungry.'

'How many meals have you been skipping? You are working hard enough for two people.'

'You said—'

'Forget what I said,' Rafael instructed, waving aside his previous comments with a regal wave of his hand. 'You are obviously not eating enough to keep a sparrow alive,' he condemned harshly.

'I eat!' she protested.

'I will believe that when I see it,' he returned smoothly.

Libby shook her head and reached for her belt. 'I'll catch the train.' She cursed softly under her breath when her trembling fingers fumbled the clip. 'I shouldn't have got in anyway. Certifiable idiot that I am I thought that... How was I to know I was your good deed for the day—?'

'Be still.'

Libby obeyed the stern caution, not out of choice, but because she couldn't not obey. She couldn't have moved if her life had depended on it, for no better reason than he was touching her. He was touching her and she had forgotten how to move.

She stared at his big hand on her lap where it imprisoned both her own hands; the slight movement of his thumb over the inner aspect of her wrist was sending hot flurries.

'*Dios*, you are shaking!'

Libby, made dizzy by his closeness, overwhelmingly aware of the clean male scent that rose from his warm body, closed her eyes.

A thoughtful expression drifted across his face. 'What did you think, Libby? Why did you think I asked you to get in the car?'

'Ask?' she echoed bitterly. 'You didn't ask, you ordered.'

'Do not try and deflect—it will not work with me. Answer me, Libby. I am not getting any younger sitting here.'

'Fine!' Libby shook her head, unable to withstand either the pressure of his questions or the pressure inside her skull. 'If you must know I thought you were going to renew your proposition.' She buried her face in her hands. 'I thought you were going to ask me to go to bed with you,' she mumbled miserably.

'And if I had what would your reply have been?'

Libby lifted her head, her expression cautious as she scanned his face. The fierce hunger she saw in his eyes drew the air from her lungs in one gasp.

The mixture of excitement and exhilaration coursing through her veins made it difficult for

Libby to force the words out. 'I would have said yes,' she admitted.

'Then I am asking.'

Libby swallowed and levelled her clear blue gaze on his face. She was shaking feverishly but her voice was steady as she whispered, 'Yes!'

At that point the voice of caution in her head threw in the towel; the only thing that Libby was listening to was the hunger roaring like an out-of-control forest fire through her veins. She didn't know if this decision was wrong but, more to the point, she didn't care—it felt right.

The look of carnal promise in Rafael's half-closed eyes sent a fresh rush of heat through her body. Libby felt weak with lust when she looked at him.

'Do not look at me like that or we might not make it to my apartment,' he growled wincing and sliding seamlessly into his own language as he crunched the gears in his eagerness to move off into the traffic.

'You make me act like a teenager.' Rafael was unaware that he voiced this rueful opinion in his native tongue. 'But I will not be clumsy in bed, *querida*, I promise you,' He added in the same tongue.

They exchanged not a word during the fifteen-minute journey to the apartment building that housed Rafael's penthouse flat. It had seemed to a frustrated Rafael that every light was against them.

To Libby, sitting silently beside him, the journey went by in a blur. She abandoned any attempt to try and rationalise what she was doing and concentrated instead on a more practical aspect of the situation.

She had just been invited into the bed of a man who was experienced and highly sexed. The subject had not come up but she was pretty sure that he was not expecting to take a clumsy, clueless virgin to bed.

Should she warn him or should she wing it? If she told him would he run a mile? Libby didn't have a clue, but why should she have any insight? She barely knew the man.

The idea of discussing anything so private horrified her, which was pretty perverse considering she was planning to share her body with him.

Libby gave up trying to see any pattern of logic in her decisions because clearly there wasn't any. It was as if she became a different person around him, one she didn't recognise.

When the lift opened into his apartment she hung back.

Rafael's patience snapped. So far she hadn't said a single word and now she stood there looking like a martyr about to be thrown to the lions.

'What is the matter?'

She shook her head. 'Nothing, I just… Is there anyone here?'

'I have no live-in staff. I am quite capable of taking care of myself. I have been doing it for a long time.'

'Oh,' she said, stepping with marginally less trepidation into the big loft-style space. 'Someone said you have a castle that's been in your family for generations. I thought—'

'You thought I needed someone to put tooth-paste on my toothbrush. And I was not brought up in any castle or even any house, just a series of...' He paused. 'My lifestyle was nomadic. The castle was my grandfather's home. I have never even visited it.'

'Nomadic—that sounds very romantic.'

The innocent remark drew a grim, hard laugh from Rafael. 'It was not,' he said bluntly. 'I had lived in five South American countries before I was twelve and nothing in any of them was.' He stopped abruptly, allowing Libby a glimpse of shock in his eyes before his luxuriant lashes swept downwards. 'It was not romantic or picturesque, but it was a good school for survival skills.' It was about the only school Rafael had gone to; he had taught himself to read and developed a ferocious appetite for the written word that had stayed with him.

Libby's rioting curiosity dried up the moment he turned to her and said casually, 'Would you like a drink or would you prefer to go straight to the bedroom?'

She started to shake her head; the glow of arousal that had brought her this far dissolved. 'That sounds so *clinical*.'

Rafael looked startled by the comment. 'What did you expect—a rose-petal path to the bed?'

His comment sent an unexpected stab of pain through Libby, who had always thought her first time would be special or at least not like this, just for sex.

'I don't know what I expected,' she admitted, biting her lips and hating the fact she was acting like a scared virgin.

You are a scared virgin.

Rafael took it for granted she shared his ability to enjoy sex just for sex… Libby was not so sure.

'Look, I'm sorry,' Rafael said, struggling to see the situation from her point of view. He did not date women to whom the courtship ritual of dinners and flowers was important. 'If I seem… I would like nothing better than spending the entire night with you, but you set the rules and I wanted to make the most of what time we have, because to be honest wanting you is driving me insane.'

Libby, recognising his attempt to understand her feelings, felt some of the tension leave her shoulders. It was also pretty flattering to be told by an incredibly sexy man that he was mad in lust with you.

'Think of it as make-up sex.'

The suggestion drew her startled gaze to his face.

'I hate to sound picky—' actually she sounded breathless '—but to have make-up sex, you have to have already had sex in the first place. Or did we and I forgot?'

Rafael's eyes lifted from her heaving bosom; his eyes burnt so hot they made Libby dizzy.

'Oh, you wouldn't have forgotten, *querida*.' His throaty purr of promise sent a fresh lick of heat through Libby's trembling body.

A nerve throbbed in his cheek as he leaned in closer, his breath stirring the sensitised nerve endings around her ear as he whispered throatily, 'And if we had already had sex this wouldn't be—my brain wouldn't be...I wouldn't be feeling—' He stopped, swallowed and thought, If we'd had sex I might be able to complete a sentence. 'All right, if you want to be pedantic let's call it make-up-for-lost-time sex.'

Save-my-sanity sex, he thought, holding his breath as he reached out. Libby froze as his fingers grazed her scalp. She was nailed to the spot by a tidal wave of enervating lust and longing. Inside her chest her heart hammered away; her mouth was dry.

Libby wanted him to touch her so much that it physically hurt. She literally ached with need that tingled under her skin like a dark flame. She moistened her lips nervously with her tongue, drawing his hungry cinnamon stare to the quivering curve.

Rafael was unprepared for the shaft of tenderness mingled in with the consuming lust as he looked at the face turned up to him, eating up the delicate perfection of her flawless cut-glass features with his hungry eyes. Her delicate blue-veined eyelids fluttered as he bent his head, brushing his lips across the surface of each in turn.

Libby gasped and her eyelids flew open just as

his fingers worked free the pins that held her hair back from her face.

Their eyes locked, Rafael straightened up. A nerve in his lean cheek pulsed, the muscles in his jaw and neck standing out taut. He watched with a satisfied smile as her hair slid in a silky cloud around her shoulders.

'Now shake your head.'

Without thinking Libby obeyed the instruction. She had a feeling she'd do pretty much anything he asked of her. She wanted to please him, which should, if she'd been in her right mind, have scared her witless.

She wasn't scared any longer, but then she definitely wasn't in her right mind.

A low growling sound of approval emerged from Rafael's throat as he watched the silky cloud bounce then settle around her face.

'Like silk,' he said, sliding his fingers into the mesh of glossy waves. 'Hot silk. *Dios*, I have been wanting to do this for ever.'

'We only met three weeks ago,' she protested, thinking, Stop talking and kiss me.

And then he was.

The kiss did not start slow and build, it just exploded. Rafael prised her lips apart with ruthless efficiency and stabbed his tongue deep into her mouth.

Her lingering doubts were blitzed away at the first touch of their lips. Libby gasped as the heat exploded everywhere; it rolled over her in waves; it burnt inside her; it prickled across the surface of her skin.

She felt the purr of approval in his throat as she wrapped her arms around his neck and kissed him back with a wild passion that matched his own. Not once during the wild kissing frenzy did she think of herself as a virgin.

She just thought, More, and closed her eyes to shut out the rest of the world.

She could do it; she was great at this—who'd have known?

When Rafael finally drew back it was to sweep her up into his arms. Supporting her weight with casual ease with one hand, he swept the hair back from her face with the other to reveal her passion-flushed features.

'You're beautiful.'

The raw wonder in his voice made her stare. It seemed miraculous to her that she could affect a man like this, that he could want her.

She looked back at him with those big eyes and Rafael felt something break loose inside him. Not even attempting to put a name to this nebulous feeling, he ran a finger down the soft curve of her cheek, fascinated by the texture of her silky skin.

Fascinated by all of her.

He wanted all of her in a way that he had never experienced with any other woman.

'So are you.'

Rafael grinned, then stopped as Libby turned her head and touched her tongue to his finger. She felt his gasp and gave a sultry smile. 'You taste good. Are you taking me to bed?'

Rafael stared at her with glowing eyes that made her think of a hungry wolf.

'That,' Rafael admitted huskily, 'is the idea, but much more of this I might not make it that far.'

Striding across the room urgently, he kicked open the door and walked straight across to the bed.

Mesmerised by the hot embers of passion glowing in his eyes, Libby pushed her face into his neck, nuzzling her way along the strong column of his throat as he strode across the room.

He dragged the duvet down and laid her on the bed.

Leaning over her, one hand either side of her face, he kissed her slowly, deeply, with an eroticism that made her stomach muscles quiver.

'Look, I really should tell you I'm not that great in bed.'

He didn't look unduly concerned by her confession. 'I like a challenge.'

Libby thought, Well, I did warn him—kind of, and arched up to him, looping her arms around his neck, sliding her fingers into his hair, then protesting a moment later when he unpeeled them and stood up.

The alarm that flared in her smoky blue eyes faded as he began to fight his way with flattering haste out of his jacket, pausing only to fling it across the room before moving on to his shirt. She watched, tongue caught between her teeth, her breath coming in a series of short choppy gasps as the fabric parted to reveal the golden hair-roughened skin of his chest and the muscled ridges of his flat belly.

The voluptuous sigh of pleasure that left her lips drew his eyes to her face. With her red hair tousled and spread across the pillow, she was the fantasy that had haunted his dreams made warm flesh.

Except for the clothes. The thought of divesting his wanton angel of those unnecessary items and revealing that lovely body for his delectation put extra urgency into Rafael's actions.

His fingers felt clumsy as he reached for the buckle on the belt of his trousers. The thought of her watching him, the thought of her growing hot for him, increased the level of his desire several more painful notches. He winced. The tailored cut of his trousers was making very little allowance for his level of arousal.

It was a relief to finally kick them away.

Libby's heart was in her mouth as he returned to join her on the bed, all lean muscle and raw strength, a rampant male at the height of his powers.

She trembled in anticipation of his touch, and not just his touch—he was wearing only a pair of boxer shorts that did little to disguise the pulsing imprint of his erection and his size exerted a shocking fascination for her.

He ran a hand down the curve of her thigh and she shivered, her nostrils flaring at the warm musky smell of arousal on his body, the carnal ache low in her pelvis deepening in response.

She touched his chest, placing her palm flat against his warm hard skin, feeling the slickness of the sweat that glossed the entire surface of his body as she spread her fingers wide.

'I can feel your heart beating.'

His burning eyes trained on her face, Rafael took her hand and, closing his fingers over hers, pressed it back on his body. His hand dragged hers in a downward sweep that followed the thin line of dark body hair that bisected his flat belly and vanished beneath the low-slung waistband of his boxers.

Holding her eyes, he pressed her hand against the bold bulge of his erection before taking her fingers and curling them around the hard column beneath the thin layer of silk.

A whimper of longing was wrenched from Libby's throat as liquid heat rushed between her thighs.

'That is what you do to me.' He released a low hiss and shook his head with regret. 'No, not yet, *querida*.' He took the hand she had slid beneath the silky barrier and raised it to his lips. 'I have not yet the control,' he confessed ruefully.

Libby stared at him, eyes mistily bright, her cheeks scored with feverish colour. She barely registered his comment; control was for her a dim and distant memory. She was looking at his dark face and found herself wanting to say, I love you.

The effort of keeping the words inside drew a moan.

'Not long,' he promised, kissing her. Libby hung

onto him, feeling herself dragged along on the tide of his white-hot passion.

She opened her mouth to the erotic exploration of his tongue, writhing as she felt his hands on her body. He seemed to know exactly where to touch her to exert the most damage to her nervous system and the most pleasure to her brain.

She heard him say her name, felt his hot breath on her face and her breast, the soft curve of her belly, and she gave herself up to the sheer sensation of it, not even registering until she felt the air on her overheated skin that he had divested her of all her clothing barring her bra and pants. Neither were designed with seduction in mind.

She spared a fleeting wistful thought for the naughty red lace set, an impulse purchase that remained unworn in the back of her wardrobe, but moments later the red lace was forgotten as he knelt above her and slid the already unclipped bra from the proud full curves of her aching breast.

His groan of male appreciation sent a primitive thrill through Libby. Eyes blazing, he reached out to cup one quivering peak and she gasped, her body arching as he followed up the caress with the brush of his tongue across the ruched rosy peak of first one breast and then the next.

Her keening cry was lost in his mouth as Rafael claimed her lips once more, the bruising quality of his kiss pushing her head back into the pillow.

She felt the strength leave her limbs as she felt him slide her pants smoothly down her thighs.

Rafael breathed hard as he stared down at the beautiful woman lying there trembling with need, the blush of desire just below the surface of her creamy skin giving it a translucent glow.

Libby looked back at him with eyes so blue they could strip a man's soul bare.

'*Madre di Dios!*' he breathed as without a word she parted her thighs in silent invitation.

Shocked by her own boldness, Libby gave a gasp as he slid a long finger along the sensitive skin of her inner thigh. Her eyes squeezed closed as she concentrated on the feather-like touch, every nerve ending stretched as he moved towards her slick heat.

'Is that for me, *querida*?' he slurred as his touch

reached the tight nub hidden by the dusting of red curls at the apex of her spread thighs.

Libby shook her head, beyond speech, incapable of anything but responding to his touch as she heard him rasp erotic sounding words in his native tongue. She did not have to understand what he was saying to find the sound of his slurred voice unbearably exciting.

The first touch of his bare flesh against her own drew a gasp of shock from Libby, who did not retreat from the searing heat of his body, but pressed herself into it, seeking to deepen the contact, that desire growing into frantic desperation as she felt the pulsing imprint of his erection against her belly.

She arched upwards, her arms wrapping themselves across his sweat-slick muscled back as he settled between her legs.

With one smooth thrust he drove deep into her body.

The sound of her shocked cry of pain would he knew stay with him for ever.

For a split second his mind emptied as he rejected the truth, for a moment he embraced the sanity-saving nothingness.

The respite was brief.

Recriminations hovered just on the edge of his consciousness but Rafael pushed them away and let himself enjoy the tight silken body holding him.

There were no words to describe the way it felt to have him inside her, stretching her, filling her.

'You're so…oh, God, Rafael…this is so… Rafael…' She repeated his name over and over, putting all her aching need and wonder into the three syllables.

'Relax,' he soothed, moving a little way deeper and feeling her gasp, then sigh. He retreated, felt her fingernails dig into his back, and repeated the process, murmuring encouragement as he felt her begin to move with him.

To know that he was the first one to give her this pleasure gave him a primitive thrill. Determined to make this first time one that she would remember, he reined in his passion, carefully controlling the thrusts of his body.

Libby closed her eyes and hung on, her face pressed into the curve of his neck, feeling the heat inside her build until it filled her, until she was the heat, then just when she thought she couldn't get any hotter everything exploded.

She heard Rafael's voice in her ear murmur, 'Go with it, angel.'

And she did, she went with it all the way, becoming part of the crashing climax that swept like a wave through her body.

Rafael felt her tighten around him, heard the cry of pleasure wrenched from her throat and felt his control slip. Helpless to hold back any longer, he buried all of himself deep inside her and felt his shattering climax claim him.

CHAPTER THIRTEEN

RAFAEL lay breathing hard, staring at the ceiling. Beside him Libby lay curled up like a kitten, her head on his chest, her thigh thrown across his hip.

'It did not cross your mind to mention the fact you were a virgin?'

Libby opened one eye, wary but taking some encouragement from his conversational tone.

'It crossed my mind,' she admitted.

'But you decided in your wisdom not to bother.'

Libby grimaced at the sarcasm in his voice and gave a non-committal grunt and trailed her fingers down the cooling skin of his chest.

Rafael caught her hand and tipped her onto her back. 'You can't distract me,' he lied.

His eyes slid down her slim body; the love-making had barely taken the edge off his hunger for her.

This, Libby thought as she peeled away from his warm body, was the hard part, one she had not really thought about until now.

'I have to go,' she said, thinking, Play it cool, Libby. He doesn't want gushing sentiment, just sex. He got that, though possibly with less finesse than he had anticipated.

Rafael lay there silently as she gathered her clothes from around the room and, standing with her back to him, began to fasten the bra across her narrow back, fumbling a little before she aligned the clasp.

'This is not how it should be the first time,' he said, his eyes on the pert curve of her deliciously rounded bottom.

The undercurrent of dissatisfaction rumbling in his voice made her turn her head.

'Do you want me to apologise? If so I'm sorry I was so crap in bed.' She arched a brow. 'Satisfied?'

'Do not be so ridiculous!'

Libby flushed and slid her skirt up over her thighs, twisting it around to reach the zip. She knew her childish response had deserved the reprimand.

He watched her struggle for a moment, then with an irritated oath vaulted from the bed and moved across to join her. 'Let me.'

Libby held herself rigid while he slid the zip up.

'I do not require an apology,' he said, not moving away. 'I require an explanation.'

Libby gave a choked little laugh. He was in for a long wait—with six feet five of magnificent rampant naked male standing next to her she was having a hard time remembering her name!

He, on the other hand, seemed totally at ease with his naked state. 'You surely did not save yourself this long to have a quick tumble then off home.' If he had known, if she had warned him... He struggled to manufacture anger and failed.

How could he be angry she had given him the most incredible sex he had ever experienced? And though it shouldn't have, the knowledge that he was her first had added to and not detracted from his post-coital pleasure.

'What was it like your first time?' Libby swallowed and dragged her gaze away from his naked body. Just looking at him sent a rush of hormonal heat through her body; the intensity of her reaction to him was almost scary.

He looked startled by the question and then frowned. 'I hardly remember,' he said vaguely, his eyes on the lacy bra as he handed her the jacket from the floor.

'You have a delicious body.'

'Thank you, so do you.' Staring at a point over his shoulder, she missed the twitch of his lips. 'I should have told you,' she admitted. 'I didn't because I thought you might have a rule…like the no-romance-in-the-office rule, a no-virgin-on-my-watch…?'

'I like to cover all eventualities but I didn't see this one coming,' he admitted.

Libby went over to the mirror on the wall, relieved to see him pull a pair of jeans from a shelf in the wardrobe that ran along one wall of the room.

She smoothed her hair with little effect. 'I've

never done this before because I've always thought I couldn't do sex without…really caring for someone.'

'But with me you can.'

'It was incredible,' she admitted. 'And I don't even like you.'

In the act of zipping up his jeans, Rafael paused.

She was aware of his scrutiny and an anxious expression slid across her face. 'I've not offended you, have I? I sometimes say things without thinking, especially when I'm tired…' She covered her mouth to hide the wide yawn she could not stop.

As he looked over at her Rafael felt his anger drain away, tipping in a direction dangerously close to tenderness; this woman was the best cure for an inflated ego he had ever come across.

'Not at all. I have no problem being treated like a sex object, outside office hours.' He pulled a white tee shirt over his head and reached for his car keys off the dresser.

'You're taking me home?'

'That was the deal. Libby…?'

She tilted her head and found him watching her with an expression she found difficult to interpret. 'Would you care to do this again?'

If her earlier remarks had bruised his ego her fervent, *'Yes, please,'* more than compensated.

The first night set the pattern for the nights to come.

At the end of each day Libby would wait by the car, they would drive to his apartment and start to tear off each other's clothes before falling into bed. It was all very intense. She wondered if this was because they were trying to cram an entire night's love-making into a short space of time.

A situation with which Rafael was openly frustrated. She had thought he might tire of the arrangement and, knowing his reputation, lose interest, but if anything his appetite was more rampant than it had been.

Libby had not lost interest either. A week after their first time she had been so consumed by her hunger for him that she hadn't been able to wait for him to undress.

She had been frantic to touch and feel him.

They had not even kissed when she had pushed him down onto the bed and, kneeling beside him, tugged down the zip of his trousers.

Freeing his engorged erection and seeing how aroused he was had only increased her levels of excitement. To hear him groan and respond to her touch had driven her delirious with hot desire.

She had not resisted the temptation to taste him, run her tongue along the throbbing length of him the way he had taught her, before taking him into her mouth. When he had finally pulled her away and, sliding her skirt up to her waist, slid into her, Libby had come so fast and hard that she had sobbed.

Afterwards she had not been able to believe she had acted that way. For the rest of the week when they had passed in the corridor she hadn't been able to look at him without imagining he was thinking of the same thing she was.

Libby hadn't lost interest; Libby was hooked; Libby was in love. The realisation had made her more inhibited. She was desperately afraid that in the grip of passion she would blurt out her feelings, which would effectively bring this idyll to an end.

Rafael had given lovers gifts before, but he always designated the task to others. This time he ventured forth into the jeweller's himself—he would know what he wanted when he saw it.

He did. He had rejected a number of items before the diamond and sapphire earrings were placed before him.

He knew immediately that they would suit Libby.

He carried them around for the entire day, anticipating her pleasure when she received them. This fantasy lasted right up to the moment that she opened them, then sat staring down at the open box with a stricken expression on her white face.

'What's wrong? Don't you like them?' Not gutted, he told himself, just disappointed she did not appreciate the value of the gift. No woman would sneer at a gift that came with the price tag these had.

'They're beautiful, but I can't accept them.' She closed the lid and pushed them back towards him.

'Why can't you accept them?' Rafael was unable to hide his annoyance.

'It feels like you're rewarding me for…for favours.'

The absurdity of the comment made him see red. He had put effort into this gift and she was throwing it back in his face, quoting stupid principles to excuse bad manners.

'I am not paying you for sex!'

'It just feels that way, sorry.'

Rafael was so furious he considered walking out, and then she produced another one of those uncensored comments that always captivated him.

'I'd pay you.' The eyes that were lifted to his face were filled with a helpless longing. 'I spend all day thinking about…' that she could still blush was both ridiculous and charming '…the time I'm with you…'

'Forget it,' he said, sliding the box into his pocket.

They spoke no more of the gift, but the following night when he handed her a brown document folder it was with the instruction not to open it.

'It is not a gift, just the deeds to the factory in your name. Not payment, simply the fulfilment of my part of our deal.'

'But that wasn't our deal—you said if I could prove I could run things you would put me in as a manager.'

He raised his brows. 'I think you misunderstood. It was always my intention to divest myself of this company to you or someone else.' He shrugged. 'It is all the same to me, but in my experience when something good falls in your lap you should not refuse it. You have heard the rumours of how I made my fortune, how I started out?'

'Some,' she admitted.

'Well, the truth is that one of my mother's… friends. My mother had many friends. This one left one night, my mother was heartbroken. It was actually several days before I found the jacket he had left behind. In the pocket there was a stone. He was a big poker player so I'm assuming that he won it in a game. I doubt he ever knew what it was. I on the other hand had read a book on diamonds. I recognised its value. It now belongs to a Russian oligarch who had it cut—one day maybe I will buy it back.'

'So you kept the stone?'

He laughed. 'Well, I did not hand it in at the local police station. It was several years later that I had it properly valued. By then my mother was dead and it gave me a chance to make something of myself.'

'You were alone?'

'I was used to looking after myself. Some of my mother's friends did not like the idea of baggage so she was asked to choose.'

Libby's heart ached for the little boy he had been who had been left behind.

'I was big and strong for my age. There were many people willing to take me in.'

Libby couldn't hide her horror. 'I can't imagine…'

'Good. I'm glad you can't—that is how it should be.'

Libby's thoughts raced. 'If I take this, does that mean that my internship is ended?'

'Do you think you have anything more to learn?'

'Of course I do!'

'Then I suggest you stay until you have learnt all the skills you require.'

Libby had no idea if he was talking bed or boardroom, she was just relieved that this wasn't ending.

It was not yet nine when his early breakfast meeting wound down. Rafael set off on foot to make his way back to the office. He was within a few hundred yards of the building when he spotted her, the brightness of her hair catching his eye, the slim curviness of her figure holding it.

He changed direction and followed her, watching as she walked into the coffee bar. He watched through the window as she headed for an empty table and took her place in the rush-hour queue.

His mood lifted at the thought of joining her. He was about to do just that when he saw a man join her. Tall and fair-haired, he bent forward speaking to her, smiling.

A chat-up line, Rafael thought, waiting with a

smile to see Libby send him packing. Only she didn't. She smiled and started chatting to him.

Rafael stood there and swore, fighting the instincts that told him to walk in there and drag the young man out.

The thought of Libby's reaction to that made his lips twitch into a reluctant smile—that would go down almost as well as chest-banging or putting an ad in a national daily announcing to the world at large that this was his woman.

Except she wasn't. They had an understanding and there was nothing in this understanding that specifically stated they were exclusive—he had just assumed.

He shook his head. He was acting as though she were kissing the guy, not passing time with her neighbour in a queue.

Rafael did not know what was wrong with him.

He was living the dream; he was enjoying the best sex of his life. He had a beautiful woman in his bed, a woman who made him laugh with no complications.

And there, he realized, lay the source of his

dissatisfaction. His nostrils flared as he forced himself to follow the train of thought through.

He wanted complications.

It was a staggering discovery.

CHAPTER FOURTEEN

'GRETCHEN?'

His PA lifted her head, saw her boss standing there and put the phone down with a rueful sigh. 'All right, I admit it was a personal call.'

'Cara?'

Gretchen nodded, encouraged by the relatively mellow response. 'Yes, it was. She needs cheering up.'

'She works at Meltons, doesn't she?'

His PA nodded. 'Worked.'

'I did wonder when I heard they were shedding that many jobs. So she's job hunting…how's it going?' Rafael was not surprised when his secretary shrugged and said gloomily, 'Not well, a trillion applications and so far nothing. If Cara with her qualifications can't get a job what chance do other people have?'

'Her expertise is IT, isn't it?'

Gretchen nodded. 'She graduated top of her class. She's brilliant or, to put it in the words of the places she applied to, over-qualified. Talk about catch-22.'

'We are expanding our IT division.'

'Yeah, I know. I sent out the job ad to the dailies.'

'Has Cara thought of applying? I'm not making any promises but—'

So astonished she knocked her neatly arranged row of ballpoint pens onto the floor, Gretchen cut across him. 'You're not sacking me, are you?'

Rafael angled an impatient look at her bent head. He knew better than to continue until she had rearranged her pens to her satisfaction. 'No, I'm not sacking you.'

'Just checking. So what about the no-romantic-involvements-in-the-workplace rule?'

'It is possible that I might be relaxing that rule,' Rafael conceded.

A slow smile spread across his PA's face as she

looked at him closely. 'If I didn't know better I'd say that was a blush.'

Rafael's white grin flashed. 'Do not push it, Gretchen,' he growled.

Gretchen, one eye on the geometric precision of the pads on her desk, grinned. 'I'll pass on the message to Cara, though I do have one worry.'

Rafael arched a questioning brow.

'As you know, Cara is a redhead and I'm a bit worried given your weakness—'

Rafael could hear her throaty chuckle as he walked down the corridor. He smiled all the way to the park where he knew that Libby ate her sandwich before he lost his nerve. Libby was not alone or eating, she was standing under the large horse-chestnut tree surrounded by her father and what he presumed was the rest of her family.

He moved off at a tangent, walking along the line of trees until he was in earshot.

It was Kate Marchant who was speaking.

'So it's true, then—you're not trying to deny it. You are sleeping with Alejandro. You're his mistress. When Rachel said she'd seen you going into his flat I felt as if—'

From where he stood Rafael saw Libby shake her head; he could not see her face or read her expression but he had no trouble hearing her response.

'No, I'm not denying it, Mum. Please,' she begged. 'Don't cry.'

'Cry? What do you expect her to do? Cheer?' her brother cried. 'Libby, that man—how could you? After what happened to Meg. Have you lost your mind?'

'What happened to Meg was not Rafael's fault.'

'So you're saying it was my fault!' her brother flared back.

Well aware that no matter what he said her brother blamed himself for allowing Meg to travel, Libby reached out to squeeze her brother's arm. 'I'm not saying it was anyone's fault—' Tears of hurt sprang to her eyes when Ed flinched away as though her touch were poison.

Her father shook his head. 'How could you betray us this way with the man who ruined me?'

'You're not ruined. With the rescue package everyone keeps their jobs and you keep the house.'

'And you expect me to be grateful.'

Libby looked at her father and thought, Yes, actually, I do.

'We are *allowed* to stay in the house like tenants in our own home, reliant on the charity of that man!'

'I know it's tough, but—!'

'You know nothing, Libby. This so-called rescue package—haven't you realised that's just a front?'

'A front?' Libby was mystified by the comment.

'A smokescreen. This isn't about charity. He jumped in with both feet wielding an axe. He can't admit he was wrong so he comes up with this *rescue package* fooling gullible people like you into thinking he's some sort of hero when in actual fact he doesn't have a clue what he's talking about.'

As she listened to the rant Libby felt growing anger. Did her father actually *believe* the stuff he was spouting?

'A man like that doesn't do anything unless there's a profit in it.'

Libby bit her lip and struggled to stay calm. 'Look, Dad, I don't want to hurt any of you.' Her heart sank as she searched their faces, recognising that her words were falling on deaf ears. It wouldn't matter what she said; their minds were closed to anything she said.

This ambush was not about listening to her explanations. They wanted remorse, they wanted penitence, and Libby knew she could give neither.

A fortnight ago, a week even, her reaction might have been different, but not now.

Now she would not apologise, she would not allow anyone to turn what she had with Rafael into anything sordid and she would not be party to any character assassination. She had made Rafael the scapegoat, blamed him for everything, but now she knew differently.

'Not want to hurt us?' Kate Marchant echoed, looking at her daughter with a coldness that hurt Libby more than she had imagined possible. 'Then you have a strange way of showing it!'

'Mum, please…'

Rafael took a step forward; the anguish in her voice felt like a blade sliding between his ribs. She looked so alone standing there that the need to protect her was too strong to resist.

'At least say you're ashamed of your dirty secret. That you're ashamed you betrayed your family.'

The words brought Rafael to a halt. Fists clenched at his sides, he waited for her reply.

'Leave her, Ed, it's not her fault. It is that man,' Kate Marchant cut in. 'He poisons everything he touches.'

'Yes, I am ashamed.'

The blood drained from Rafael's face. It was no more than he expected, he told himself. Why should it hurt? He had been rejected before and survived.

Libby lifted her chin proudly. 'I'm ashamed that I ever was ashamed. I'm ashamed that I asked Rafael to keep our affair a secret. I'm not ashamed now, I'm proud. He deserves a lot better, a lot better than me. None of those things that you think about him are true. He's an incredible person, he's overcome so many things and…the people who work for him—do you think it's accidental that they'd do anything for him? Go see for yourselves. You won't hear anyone say a bad word about him, not the ones that know him.'

'Do you think it's possible that they're worried this saint might sack them?' Ed asked drily. He gave a snort of disgust and shook his head.

Her family stared in varying degrees of horror as she maintained her defiant stance.

'Look what he did to your father, Libby,' Kate Marchant inserted. 'You know what sort of man he is.'

'Grow up, Libby,' her brother advised harshly. 'The man's having sex with you, of course he won't let you see his vicious side, but once he's got tired of you just wait and see how nice he is then.'

He turned to their parents and pointed a finger towards Libby. 'The man has brainwashed her.'

'No, Ed, he's not brainwashed me.'

'This has got to stop now,' her father said sternly.

'You have to promise us that you never see this man again.'

'Don't ask me to choose between him and you, Dad,' Libby pleaded.

Rafael watched. Taking a knife to the heart would have been easier than watching her pain.

Her family began to move away together, turning away from her, offering one another the support they had denied Libby. As much as he despised their actions today he knew that he would have to put personal feelings aside to make this thing right.

'I brought lunch but I see you've already eaten.'

Libby stared at the tall figure who stepped out from the shadow of a tree, a lunch bag rather improbably swinging in his hand. Her immediate impulse was to walk straight into his arms. There were several flaws in this plan, not least the possibility they would not open wide to enfold her the way they did in the scene playing in her head, so she fought the impulse and stayed where she was.

'Since when did you take alfresco lunches?'

'I'm always open to new experiences, embrace them even.' He glanced at the bag in his hand. 'This represents quite a big new experience for me.'

Libby barely registered the odd inflection in his voice; she had to know. She jerked her head towards the now empty bench where sparrows were dive-bombing the remains of her own forgotten lunch.

'You heard that, didn't you?'

Rafael swallowed and nodded.

Libby loosed a mortified groan and dropped her chin into her chest. 'You weren't meant to,' she mumbled miserably.

'I can't be the cause of a rift between you and your parents, Libby.'

She gave a teary smile but there was an air of finality to Libby's response. 'You can't stop me, Rafael, unless you are saying you want this…us to stop.'

'Families are important.' She had something that he did not; he could not let her throw it away.

Libby looked at him, loving every line of his proud face. He was her family. Pity he didn't know.

'I know families are important. I love my family, Rafael, but they needed to know—'

'Needed to know what?'

'The truth,' she said, talking to his tie now.

He ran a finger down the curve of her cheek and said softly, 'Look at me, Libby.'

Libby lifted her gaze.

'They were angry. They did not mean the things they said, you know. Your family loves you.' If making them value what they had meant he had to force-feed them a few home truths, Rafael was more than prepared to perform this task.

Libby swallowed and thought, Why can't you? She pushed away the wistful thought. She had to accept what she could not have and enjoy what she could.

God, it *sounded* so easy!

'I know they do. And I love them.' The difference was she wasn't asking them to prove it.

'If you are estranged from your family, eventually, not today perhaps or even next week, but the time will come when you will blame me.'

Libby shook her head in rejection of his theory. 'That isn't true!' she insisted fiercely.

'Go to them, say what they need to hear, take their side. I will be fine with it.'

'Fine with us not…' Libby, ghostly pale, struggled to keep the tremor from her voice as she said huskily, 'So you're saying that you don't want us to…'

Rafael dragged a hand through his hair and stared at her as though she had lost her mind. '*Madre di Dios*, of course that is not what I'm saying.'

Libby, weak with relief, sighed. 'Then what are you saying?'

'Say what they want to hear, say you have seen the light and I am the Antichrist, and we can continue to be discreet.'

'Lie, you mean. Hide in a corner and feel cheap, as though we're doing something wrong, you mean?' Her voice cracked as she asked miserably, 'Is that what *you* want?' If it was all she could get Libby was willing to take it, but not without trying for more first.

She took a step back in order to study his face her hands twisted in a white-knuckled knot on her chest.

Rafael swore and shook his head, not looking at her directly as he growled, 'Of course it is not what I want.' He wanted to shout from the roof-tops that she was his. 'But the situation requires compromise,' he said, struggling to think past the need pounding in his skull.

Libby leaned back, pressing her head against the bark of the tree trunk as she laughed. '*You*, compromise? Since when?' she jeered shakily.

His glowing eyes raked her face, his lips twist-ing into an ironic smile as he said bitterly, 'Since I met you.'

Libby stilled, something in his face making her heart rate pick up.

'I was never the one who wished to keep this affair secret, and that has not changed,' Libby heard him say, and thought, *I have.*

'Perhaps in time your parents will—'

'In time you will have moved on to someone else!' Her fear slipped out unchecked… She closed her eyes; could she sound more needy?

A look of utter amazement crossed his face. 'That is not going to happen. How can you think that?'

'How can I not think that? Because you are so renowned for your long-term relationships! Look,' she added, struggling for some degree of composure. 'I'm not complaining. You never pretended it was anything other than it was.'

'I was an idiot!'

The contempt in this observation made her blink.

From where she was standing Libby could feel the tension rolling off his big body.

'The thing you did—'

She watched him swallow and was utterly amazed to realise that Rafael, the epitome of cool, was struggling for composure.

'What thing?' she prompted gently.

'Lose something you value greatly—that you are willing to do that for me, it means…' He pressed a clenched fist to his chest and turned his head jerkily away. Libby could see the muscles in his brown throat working as he swallowed.

There was a space of several nerve-shredding seconds before he turned back. 'It means a great deal, but I cannot let you lose your family because of me.'

'I won't, but I can't let them make me lose you, Rafael.' Her heart was in her eyes as she lifted her chin and declared, 'I love you…' She saw his stunned expression and groaned. 'Oh, God, I wasn't going to say that, and you don't have to look so horrified—I won't say it again. Honestly,' she promised, miming a zipping motion across her lips. 'We can just go on the way we were and—'

A nerve clenched along his lean jaw. 'No, there is no question of us going on as we were.'

Libby caught her trembling lip between her teeth. 'That's it, then.' As her shimmering blue gaze moved across the hard planes and sculpted contours of his face Libby experienced a sudden violent surge of rebellion. She couldn't give up on something this good—not without a fight.

'No, that's *not* it!'

He arched a brow. 'It isn't?'

'You *should* want me, Rafael Alejandro. I'm a good person and I'm good for you, and one day you'll regret sending me away,' she charged huskily. 'Do you hear me?'

The blaze died from her eyes when, as suddenly as it had flared, the defiance burning inside her drained away. Her body slumped in defeat like a puppet whose strings had been severed. She looked at the accusing finger she had stabbed into his chest; it had made as little impression as her words.

'Nobody is going anywhere.' Rafael caught the finger she waved at him and, pulling it to his lips, kissed it, then applied the same treatment to each fingertip, then the palm of her hand, holding her eyes as he did so. 'Say it again!' he growled.

The autocratic demand made her blink. 'What?'

Rafael slid his hands down her shoulders and hauled her casually towards him. 'You heard me, *querida.*'

The fiercely tender glow in his eyes stole her

breath away. 'What do you want me to say?' she whispered hoarsely.

'Say you love me. I want…I *need* to hear you say it.' His implacable golden stare burned into her.

Libby couldn't tear her fascinated gaze from the nerve throbbing in his lean cheek. Her head was spinning. Was this really happening?

'I love you, Rafael.' She cleared her throat and added in a louder voice, 'I love you, I really do…I—'

The rest of her impassioned declaration was lost in the warm recesses of his mouth. Having her warm vital body in his arms, her arms curled around his neck, feeling her soft breasts plastered up against his chest, all the things he had been aching for, snapped the frayed threads of Rafael's control.

A moan was wrenched from deep inside the vault of his chest, but a second later he pulled back breathing hard.

'What just happened?' What was happening?

'If you do not know I am definitely losing my touch.'

'You're not.'

The feeling in her voice raised a smile, but a moment later it was gone and Rafael was staring at her with a fixed bone-stripping intensity that made Libby feel dizzy.

'You don't mind—about me…you know?'

Her awkward shrug raised a tender smile from Rafael, whose eyes had not left her face for a moment.

'I…' He stopped and said abruptly, 'I missed you.' Coward, said the voice in his head.

It was an accusation he could not deny. Was he ready to take that leap of faith and say the word that changed everything?

The word that meant dropping walls he had spent a lifetime building, walls that Libby had been removing brick by brick since she had exploded so dramatically into his life. Libby's influence had infiltrated every aspect of his life and heart shining light into all the dark corners and, he realized, freeing him from the self-imposed limits.

Libby blinked. 'You only saw me this morning.' Her eyes fell. It had been the first time she had woken up in his arms. She had hated the subterfuge necessary to allow her to stay the night, but it had been worth it. Of course in the end ironically the lies had been wasted; her family knew.

At least she wouldn't have to lie the next time and invent excuses—always supposing there was a next time? Rafael's reaction to her rash declaration of love had not been what she had expected, but it had not been as she had secretly hoped either. Her head ached with the effort of trying to work out what was happening.

'I want to see you every morning.'

Libby stared at him, a look of astonishment frozen on her face. 'Are you asking me to move in with you?'

'I'm...' With a frustrated groan he gathered her to him. 'No, I'm not asking you to move in with me.' He felt her stiffen in his arms and begin to pull away. 'No!' he said and tightened his grip. 'I am not doing this well. *Dios*, but you are beautiful!'

She looked at his face, his golden skin glistening with the moisture that dusted it, and felt dizzy with lust and love. 'You are the most beautiful thing I have ever seen, Rafael.'

Rafael looked startled by the fierce declaration and then smugly pleased.

'What I have been trying to say…what I came here to say is…come…!'

A totally bemused Libby responded to the imperious command and allowed him to take her hand and drag her back to the bench she had been sitting on to eat her lunch. Ignoring the two young women who were now sitting on one end, Rafael pushed her down onto the wooden seat.

Libby watched, her bewilderment growing as he unfolded the seal of his lunch bag and tipped the contents in his palm before extending his hand to her.

'I'm not actually hungry, Rafael.' Then she saw the small velvet case sitting in his palm and her throat dried, allowing nothing but a small whimper to escape.

Unable to allow herself to abandon caution, believe the message the joyous pounding of her heart was beating out, she shook her head slowly from side to side.

'What,' she asked, her voice barely more than a throaty whisper as she forced the words past the aching lump in her throat, 'is that?'

Rafael dragged a frustrated hand across his sable hair. He had always understood that women instinctively knew about such things. 'Open it and see,' he urged.

'Open it!' echoed the girl sitting the other end of the bench before her companion hushed her.

Libby's hand was shaking as she took the box from his palm. Slowly, hardly breathing, she opened it. Her eyes widened to their fullest extent when she saw the square cut sapphire surrounded by equally impressive diamonds sitting in the velvet bed.

Watching her, every clenched muscle and

stretched nerve ending in his body taut and screaming for release, he waited for her to react.

'If you don't like it I can…'

Her eyes flew to his face, the sparkle in them putting the sapphire she took carefully from the box to shame. 'It's beautiful, Rafael.'

'Marry me, Libby.'

Libby's hand went to her mouth.

A sigh lifted Rafael's chest. 'Say something!' he pleaded. Then, thinking better of the instruction, added, 'But not if it's no, Libby, don't say no.' He took her hand and slid the ring on it. 'Take the ring, take me, Libby.'

At the other end of the bench someone began to clap and a voice said, 'For God's sake, say yes!'

All Libby heard was the pain in his voice and she hated it. She leaned forward and framed his beautiful face between her hands. 'I want to say yes,' she admitted. 'I'm totally crazy about you, but I'm scared…' she whispered.

'I'm not, for the first time in my life I'm not scared, Libby, and you did that for me.' He took her hands from around his face and brought them to his lips. 'I'd turned my weakness into virtue. I took pride in not needing anyone,' he admitted with a self-contemptuous shake of his head. 'I was afraid to give anything of myself, afraid of being hurt, then you came along, so brave, so loving...' His smouldering glance moved across her tear-stained face. 'You gave me so much and I took... Let me give now, Libby.' He watched her luminous eyes fill with tears and said, 'Let me give you my heart.'

A broken sob left her throat. She knew how much this had cost; she knew about his deep-seated fear of rejection.

'Yes, Rafael, I will marry you.'

CHAPTER FIFTEEN

LIGHT shone through the shuttered Georgian windows of the bedroom Libby had slept in the previous night. Like the rest of the rooms she had seen in the beautiful country house that Rafael had taken over for the wedding, it was filled with sweet-smelling flowers and furnished with taste and style.

Her only complaint with the accommodation was that she had spent the last night in the large bed alone. Rafael, who proved to have some surprisingly traditional views on the subject, had absented himself from the room despite her protests. Admittedly he had softened the blow when he had promised her it would be the last night they would ever be spending apart.

'I cannot function without you beside me.'

Recalling the raw sincerity in his voice made Libby's eyes fill with emotional tears.

She could not believe how good her life was; perfect—well, almost. The almost brought a shadowed sadness to her blue eyes. The only cloud on Libby's horizon was the conspicuous absence of her family on her wedding day.

Every attempt she had made to contact them had been ignored, and the only response she had received to the wedding invitations and the covering letter begging them to come had been a noisy silence.

For Rafael's sake she had put a brave face on it, knowing that he continued to feel responsible for the situation. She had told him she was sure that they would come around eventually, but as the days had passed her optimism was becoming more forced.

Libby pushed away the dark thoughts and, picking up the skirt of her long gown off the polished wood floor in one hand, she moved towards the open door to join her friends.

At the last moment she paused and turned back to glance for one last time at her reflection in the antique cheval mirror.

She barely recognised the young woman standing there looking back at her. She touched the beaded bodice of the exquisite dress she wore, glad now that she had allowed her better judgment to be overruled by Susie, who had flown over from New York the previous week to be her bridesmaid.

Her outspoken friend had not minced her words when Libby had said with regret that the deceptively simple cream gown was far too expensive.

'Too expensive!' she'd hooted derisively. 'Give me a break, Libby!'

'This isn't going to be a big wedding, Susie.' Rafael had at her request scaled back his plans when she had said she hadn't wanted the day to be too big and impersonal.

'What has size got to do with it? You want to knock his socks off, don't you?' She'd sensed Libby wavering and pushed home her advantage. 'In that dress it is job done. Unless of course he's short of cash, is he?'

'No, but—'

'But nothing, you're marrying a billionaire who

is utterly besotted with you. What did you think he had in mind when he flies us over to Paris in a private jet—that you rummage through the charity shops for a bargain?'

She had waved a hand towards the rail of couture wedding gowns that had been produced when the style consultant who had met them at the airport had dropped the bridegroom's name.

'No, of course not, but there are some really nice ones that don't cost—'

'You don't expect eighty metres of hand-embroidered Paris couture to come cheap,' Susie had pointed out.

When Libby had continued to hesitate she had planted her hands on Libby's shoulders and steered her back to the mirror. 'Is that perfect or is it perfect?'

'Phoebe thinks that the—'

'Do you want to be dressed by a fashion consultant?'

'It is perfect, isn't it?'

It had been and it still was, Libby admitted, turning to see the effect of the elegant train when she moved. The long tendrils left free of the simple knot of curls on her head brushed softly against her cheek as she moved.

With one last smiling look at the girl in the mirror she turned and walked into the other room.

'Drum roll,' she cried, striking a pose. 'What do you think?'

The two women stopped talking and turned in unison. When neither said a word a flicker of uncertainty appeared in Libby's face.

'I thought I looked *quite* nice?' She tried to hide her bitter disappointment behind a rueful smile. She really had hoped for slightly more positive feedback than this. 'You think I should have gone with the hair down?'

Libby expected a response to her question but not this one. Her eyes widened in astonishment when her maid of honour Chloe suddenly burst into tears and even tough cookie Susie's eyes looked suspiciously moist as she let out a silent whistle and said with feeling, 'He's going to think he's died and gone to heaven when he sees you!'

'Oh, Libby,' Chloe said, dabbing her eyes. 'You

look fabulous…like a sexy angel. Oh, no, is my mascara running?'

'Don't worry, it's waterproof,' Libby said, her ego boosted by this ringing endorsement. 'Angels don't have ginger hair,' she joked.

'That tiara is fantastic,' Susie, pretty in soft pink, enthused as she tilted her head to get a better look at the pearls and diamonds that glittered against Libby's auburn hair. 'Well, this is it, kid,' she said softly. 'You ready for this?'

Libby took a deep breath. 'I've never been more ready for anything in my life,' she said simply.

A knock on the door heralded the arrival of Chloe's husband, who had stepped up to the mark when requested to walk her down the aisle.

'Why, Joseph,' Libby teased. 'You scrub up really well.'

Joe grinned and touched his slicked-back hair. 'I feel like a total prat,' he admitted, stretching out an arm for Libby. 'But I'm guessing no one is going to be looking at me. You look very beautiful. You all do.'

'Good recovery, Joe,' his wife murmured, hand-ing Libby the bouquet of stephanotis and white roses. She smoothed down the velvet ribbon bound around the stems and stood back to see the full effect.

'Perfect.'

Her heart was beating fast as they approached the open doors of the ballroom where the guests were seated. A few feet short of the door Joe paused; she looked at him questioningly when a figure stepped out from behind a pillar.

'Dad!'

Her father smiled, and nodded to Joe, who stepped back smiling.

'Libby, my dear, you look stunning.'

'You came. I can't start crying now—it'll ruin my make-up.'

Chloe produced a tissue and Libby accepted it with a watery grin.

'I doubt if the bridegroom would care. I think that man would do anything for you, Libby. He made us see sense and I'm grateful to him for it.'

'And I'd do anything for him,' she admitted without hesitation. 'Is Mum…?'

'Everyone is here, Libby.'

The wedding march music struck up and Libby experienced a moment's panic until her father's hand tightened on her arm and Chloe, ever practical, held out her hand for the used tissue.

Behind her Libby heard Susie say, 'Camera, lights, action, you're on, Libby!'

Libby smiled at her father and walked towards the open doors. Heads turned as she entered, including those of her family. Libby smiled at them, then turned her attention to the tall figure waiting for her.

Their eyes connected and for Libby the rest of the room vanished; her eyes shone with the love that filled her eyes with tears as she walked towards him.

Later several people commented on how serene and calm the beautiful bride had sounded when she delivered her vows, while a few mentioned with knowing smiles the emotional tremor in the groom's voice and the glow of fierce pride in his eyes as he slid the ring onto his beautiful bride's finger. All were in agreement that the simple ceremony had been wonderful and the couple were stunning.

Before the wedding breakfast Libby had a few moments alone with her family. It was a very emotional reunion. She did not question their sudden decision to attend but she had her suspicions.

She challenged Rafael when they stole a moment together away from their guests.

'I know you had something to do with them being here.'

His enigmatic smile gave nothing away.

'I don't know how you did it, but thank you, Rafael.' She reached up and pressed a kiss to his lips.

Her glowing smile made Rafael feel dizzy. For the hundredth time that day he told himself he was the luckiest man alive. 'I would like to take the credit, but I did have help. Meg has been my ally in this. She has been working on the inside, so to speak.'

'Bless her,' Libby said fondly.

'My role was to charm them into submission.'

'Typecasting, but you must have been very charming.'

Rafael bared his teeth in a rueful grin. 'Actually things did not go strictly to plan. You'd looked so unhappy when I left that morning. I know you said you just felt a bit queasy but I knew you were thinking about your family.

'All the way down there I couldn't get your little face out of my head so instead of being conciliating I was quite angry, but as it happens tough love worked so I am the hero of the piece. If not I would have been the villain.'

'When you say tough love...?' she asked, amused by his candour.

'I said that they could be as angry with me as they wished, but that I would not tolerate them making you unhappy and by doing so they were effectively losing the chance to be part of their future grandchildren's lives.'

'Funny you should say that...'

Rafael arched a brow.

'The grandchildren part.'

He sighed, but appeared philosophical when he said, 'You are annoyed with me—you think I went too far?'

'No, it's not that. You see, I really was sick that morning, and then yesterday when I was with Chloe I…well, I said it was nerves but she…well, she gave me a testing kit and I used it.'

Rafael, who had struggled to follow this rambling narrative, shook his head. 'I do not follow.'

Libby sighed. 'A pregnancy-testing kit.'

She watched the comprehension spread across his face; he looked stunned. 'You are pregnant.' His eyes fell to her slim waist.

She met his eyes and nodded.

Libby felt a surge of relief when she saw the smile in his marvellous eyes. 'I am going to be a father.'

'Not for another eight months,' she warned. 'Time to get used to the idea?'

His golden eyes skimmed her upturned features. 'Libby,' he chided, stroking her cheek with a loving finger. 'You were not sure if I'd be pleased?'

'Well, it wasn't something we planned…'

'I didn't plan to fall in love. I didn't plan to marry.' He gave a fierce smile that made her pulse leap and pressed a kiss to her lips. 'I do plan to love this baby and cherish him just as I cherish his mother.'

The raw sincerity in his voice made her eyes fill with emotional tears. 'Hormones,' she sniffed.

'You are adorable,' he said, kissing the tip of her pink nose. 'And very beautiful. Our baby will be—'

'About the baby, Rafael,' she said, catching his arm. 'As it's early days and sometimes things happen…do you mind if we don't tell anyone else just yet?'

Rafael studied her face and felt a soul-piercing stab of tenderness. He knew only time would banish the doubts he saw in her eyes. 'It will be our little secret,' he agreed, laying a hand on her stomach.

'Not much of a secret if you do that in front of

people.' Despite her complaint she did not try to move his hand. She liked the feel of it there; it made her feel safe and loved.

As they strolled back to their guests a little while later Rafael looked up at the grand building. 'So this place—you like it?' he said casually.

'It's beautiful. We could actually have spent our honeymoon here, not that I'm complaining,' she added quickly, anxious to reassure Rafael that the effort he had gone to to make their honeymoon special was appreciated. 'Who would? A month on our own desert island! No shoes, no suits.' Libby slid a smiling look at the man beside her, who was looking rather magnificent in his.

Rafael, who had been looking thoughtful, added, 'No clothes.'

An image of her gorgeous husband striding along a sun-kissed beach stark naked flashed into her head and Libby blushed.

'Well, I suppose if it's private…?'

'Oh, it is private, *querida*. I have no intention of sharing you with anyone. I am glad you like it here. I was hoping you would when I bought it.'

Libby's jaw dropped. 'You what?'

'I bought the estate. This,' he said with a gesture that took in the rolling parkland, 'is your wedding gift. It is in reasonably good condition though, obviously,' he conceded, 'you will wish to make some changes décor-wise and so forth, put your own stamp it.'

'You're serious.'

'I wanted a home to bring you back to. A home is something I have never had before, something I never expected to have.'

'God, I'm going to cry again. I love the house,' she promised. 'But I'd love a tent if you were in it. Oh, God,' she said, taking the tissue he offered. 'I just love you!' she cried.

Rafael took his time to convince her that her feelings were very reciprocated.

* * * * *